# LOVING *the* TEXAS

# LAWMAN

# Garrison's Law

## BOOK 1

# MARY CONNEALY

Interior Format

# CHAPTER ONE

*Long Pine, Texas*

"AND SO, IN THE COURSE of our studies, we'll learn how we can use kindness as an effective response to anger." Trudy Jennings looked out at the sea of eyes intently watching her and felt a moment of pride. All of her students seemed genuinely interested in what she had to say.

A snort from Ben Garrison turned into a cough.

All except one.

Garrison reached for his black Stetson, which he'd set politely on the desk at the beginning of class, put it on, and pulled it low over his eyes while his shoulders shook.

Trudy clenched her jaw and attempted a tight smile, ignoring his childish antics. "We'll find out that turning the other cheek doesn't necessarily invite a second slap."

This time, even with his hat pulled low, he grabbed a handkerchief out of the inside pocket of his blazer and covered his grinning mouth. *What was the man's problem?*

She'd been putting up with his nonsense for nearly three hours during this one-night-a-week class. Her patience was gone. "What is it *this* time, Detective Garrison?"

"Nothing, Miss…uh, Dr. Jennings." He coughed again. "Got a little cold is all." He choked on the word *cold*. His shoulders shook with laughter. Between the hat and the handkerchief, he very conveniently covered his whole face.

Trudy ran a finger around the turtle-neck collar of her beige sweater to let out steam. The fact that the man was seriously trying to control himself only made it worse.

During the ice-breaker Trudy scheduled for the first fifteen minutes of class at the beginning of each semester, Ben Garrison had introduced himself as a Long Pine police detective. Detecting what, she wondered. Kindergarteners cheating at tag? She'd nicknamed him Cough Man after the first half hour.

"I'm...fine." His broken reassurance wasn't cooling her temper.

She finished her overview of how passive intervention could assist in anger management while she fought to manage her own anger.

Mr. Garrison cleared his throat suspiciously a couple of times. He sat there, slumped down, his face mostly covered by his broad brimmed hat. He wore dark pants and a white shirt with snaps, a cowboy style. A black blazer, too, and a pair of black Tony Lama boots. He said earlier he'd come straight from work.

"That's it for today. Class dismissed." She dropped her glasses in the inside breast pocket of her brown tweed blazer and ran a hand over her ponytail, pulled tight and held in place at the nape of her neck by a rectangular gold clip, nearly invisible in her golden blonde hair.

As the youngest tenured professor at Bella Vista Christian College, she did her best to appear mature and in control. She dressed to support that image, right down to her glasses, which were plain glass. Her baby blues worked just fine, thank you very much.

All the seniors in the Psych Department needed her class to graduate and they knew it. That helped her keep things under control. But it looked like this semester Mr. Garrison wasn't going to make that easy.

As her students filed out, she turned her back on the emptying room to pack her briefcase. The letter she'd tucked in with her other papers caught her eye. Turning it over, she wondered why Mr. Watson hadn't followed her advice.

She flipped the envelope open and slid the lined notebook paper out. This wasn't his first pathetic cry for help. He'd been writing nearly all summer since he'd approached her to counsel him and his estranged wife.

Over the months, his handwriting had deteriorated to an almost unreadable scrawl and his desperation grew with each letter, this one had an almost threatening tone. She re-read it with a sense of dread as he raged at her, demanding help.

'*You're the only one who can help me. You WILL help me!!! I won't stop, I won't! I'll keep coming until you give me what I want. You'll give me what I want or I'll take it!*' R Watson

The words filled a full-sized sheet of white printer paper. Some were two inches tall, underlined, scratched out and rewritten. Exclamation points. A signature that was next thing to illegible. The T that was crossed in Watson slashed through his whole name twice, obliterating it.

He'd come to her office a few times then, when she refused to see him anymore, he began writing letters. He'd sent one daily for two weeks. Each had a more fanatical tone. The paper was torn in places under the heavy lines of ink that spoke of a violent temper. All of it went together to chill her blood.

A hand closed on her shoulder.

She shrieked and whirled around. Cough Man stood inches behind her.

She staggered back. He backed away quickly. "Sorry," he said. "I didn't mean to startle you." All of his buffoonery gone, replaced with sharply intelligent, observant eyes that went right to her letter. The oversized, darkly written words visible.

She noted his instinct to protect, the cop eyes flicking from the note in her hand to her eyes.

"Are you all right?"

"I'm fine, Mr. uh…Detective Garrison. A little..uh, that is… fine."

"No, you're not." His Texas drawl sharpened and he quit studying her and turned those suspicious cop eyes to Watson's note. "What's that?"

Some reflex made her quickly fold the letter and hold it away from him.

"I said I'm fine." She spoke too sharply.

His blue eyes flickered between her face and the letter. There was none of the school-boy antics about him now. He was all homicide detective.

And he knew there was more. With an expression that said he didn't like it, he shrugged. "Okay, um…I came up here to…to…I," he threw his hands wide. "I apologize, Dr. Jennings, for my behavior in class. It's just that your lecture..."

He shook his head, then shook it harder and jammed one hand into his short, dark curls and knocked his hat off his head. He caught it and held against his belly, running his hands along the brim. "Today of all days..."

She controlled the urge to smooth the mess he'd made of his hair. He'd really be good looking if he wasn't such a pest. The lines around his analytical blue eyes were too deep for a man his age. She heard the sincerity in his apology and the exhaustion behind it.

*Today of all days.* She wondered what had happened, thought of the letter in her hand and could relate.

"Your remarks on anger management just caught me on a bad day. If I'd turned the other cheek to the guy I arrested today I'd be dead." He shook his head and looked through her into the day he'd just had. "That's the reason, but it's no excuse. My behavior in class was inexcusable."

Trudy had to admit it was a genuine apology. She'd had a lot of badly behaved students who never managed one of those. Of course, most of them were fifteen years younger than Detective Garrison.

"Honest, if I get sent to the principal's office and they call my mom in, I'll never live it down at the precinct." His blue eyes sparked with good humor, and that eased some of the cynical lines etched on his face. "Especially since Mom and Dad are on a cruise to Alaska and won't be home for two weeks. Slow time at the ranch."

"You're from a ranch family, Detective Garrison?" Her eyes flickered to the black felt Stetson he now held in both hands. This was Texas, plenty of people wore Stetsons, and they weren't all cowboys.

"Yep, my family's been ranching in Texas since before the Civil War. Dozens of Garrison cousins own land between here and Fort Worth."

"I envy you a large family, Detective. I hope you appreciate them."

"Don't you have a big family?"

It was too personal a question, and a real answer held too much pain. She said, "One great aunt retired to Florida."

Then she changed the subject. "Why aren't you ranching?"

"My branch of the family leaned more toward the military and law enforcement. But the ranch I grew up on is still home." Detective Garrison gave her a full-on smile.

She blinked at the pure wattage of it.

"I can see it now, a chopper picking up mom—better known as Hangin' Judge Janet Garrison."

"Your mom is called…" Trudy swallowed and looked a little closer at Detective Garrison. How upset would the judge be if she expelled Sonny Boy here from school? "She got that name for being stern with her children?"

"Well, no. That's not where she got it but it works at home, too. She got it on the job. She's really a judge. She's a sweetie compared to Dad. You've gotta be tough to ranch in Texas. A chopper will have to pick them up off the deck of the ship and bring them back to Fort Worth to get me out of the principal's office."

Tempted to smile at the man who had to be thirty-two or three…or five, she tightened her mouth. "Well, since we don't have a principal, Cough…uh…Mr. Garrison, you're probably in the clear. Apology accepted. I'll see you next week in class. Don't forget to read my book '*Tru Intervention: Anger Management*'."

Becoming a professor and establishing tenure at Bella Vista at such a young age was due to the success of her series of pop-psychology self-help books. She and many others across the country used them as textbooks. They were considered light-weight, she knew that, but they held Biblical wisdom. Few people noticed the source, but they were drawn to the wisdom.

"We'll be reviewing some new models for a passive, loving approach to people with rage issues."

A smile curved his lips but he quickly suppressed it. "Passive approach to rage issues." He cleared his throat. "Got it."

He turned far too quickly, settled his hat on his head with smooth, practiced ease, and left the room at a brisk pace.

Trudy could almost describe it as running.

She heard him coughing in the hall.

She crushed Watson's letter in her hand, then her shoulders slumped.

It was going to be a long semester.

Throwing the letter in her briefcase, she snapped it shut, gath-

ered up her books and left the classroom. She had to lock the
room and the whole building behind her. She was always the last
one out on Monday nights and even the long August summer
days were fully dark by ten o'clock. She flipped off each light she
passed. The hallway falling dark seemed to pursue her. Her footsteps echoed in the empty building. She realized she was reacting
to Watson's unsettling note.

Stepping outside, the heavy glass door locked automatically with
a muted click. She turned around to make sure it latched.

Pounding footsteps coming at her jerked her around. A dark
shape in the murky street lights rushed at her.

She screamed and staggered back, hitting the glass door.

Strong hands grabbed at her shoulders, clawing her blazer. She
squirmed against his grappling hands, staggered sideways and came
up against brick. Forced against the building, she screamed.

The man made vicious barely human sounds as she struggled.

"I need you." Heavy hands caught the lapels of her blazer. His
sweaty cheek slid across her face. The stench nearly choked her.
Shaggy black hair hung across his low forehead. Grunting with the
effort of subduing her, he blasted her with fetid breath.

He pressed his face against hers as he growled, "Give me what I
want, or I'll take it."

"Take...take anything you want. My briefcase...you can have it.
My wallet—"

"I don't want your money. I want you." He shook her. Her
books and briefcase tumbled to the ground, scraping her legs as
they dropped. The man kicked the books aside and caught her on
the shin with heavy boots.

"You're coming with me." His coarse voice crawled up her spine.

"No! Stop!" Jerking against his grip, she broke free again for a
second. He caught her. The left side of her face smacked against
the brick wall with a dull thud. Streaks of light exploded behind
her closed eyes. She begged God to protect her.

"I won't stop. Never."

"Help!" Trudy screamed into the empty night.

The attacker slid his hands to her throat and cut off her scream.

# CHAPTER TWO

THE NEXT SECOND, TRUDY WAS free.

She sank to the ground, and scrambled sideways on her hands and knees, sobbing as she moved away from her wild-eyed assailant. She looked over the man's shoulder and saw what had happened.

Or, rather, *who* had happened.

Ben Garrison. One muscled arm was wrapped around the maniac's neck.

All her terror faded as she looked into the policeman's eyes, cold as ice, but with so much strength and competence, the cold glare actually warmed her.

"Are you all right, Dr. Jennings?" Detective Garrison's arm tightened around his captive's neck as if a negative answer from her would be taken out on her attacker.

"Yes." Trudy's head swam and her knees shook until she didn't know if they would hold her. She scrambled to her feet, leaning heavily on the building. "I'm f...fine. He didn't hurt me."

"You can't do this." The disheveled man said, struggling against Garrison's arm. "I need her. She's coming with me. She has to help me or I'll..."

"I'm Detective Ben Garrison, Long Pine PD. This is resisting arrest." Garrison switched his hold to a hammerlock. "You're already in trouble for assault and attempted kidnapping. Her clothing is torn and, if you've got any priors, that'll be enough to tag on sexual assault. If you want to make it worse by resisting arrest, I'm all for it."

"No," the man croaked.

The visceral satisfaction of hearing the man struggle to breathe went so deep, it shocked her. Her rage stiffened her scraped knees as she came closer to the two men, careful not to get within arm's length.

"Do you know this man, Doctor?" the detective asked quietly, as if holding down the wriggling man took very little effort.

"You're...you're Ralph Watson." Trudy recognized him in the dim light. She'd only met a few times last spring before she'd told her secretary to not let him into her office again. Then he was well-dressed. He'd been desperate to persuade her to take his case but he hadn't come off as deranged.

*But his letters had.*

"Yes, I'm a patient of yours," Watson said, jerking against Ben's iron grip. "Let me go. I'm just talking to my doctor."

"I am *not* your doctor." With trembling hands, Trudy pulled her blazer onto her shoulders. "I specifically said I couldn't help you, Mr. Watson. Dr. Pavil told me you never kept your appointment with him." Trudy shook her head and her barrette swatted her in the face.

She grabbed at her hair clip, and removed it. Heavy lengths of her hair had been ripped loose and dangled from the clip. She put her hand up to her cheek and felt wet, raw skin. She remembered scraping her face on the building. She pulled her fingers away from the tender spot and shuddered at the crimson stains on them.

Trudy looked at the distraught man. "You've been sending me letters. I've also gotten some strange unsigned emails. Are those from you, too?"

Watson's sullen eyes narrowed and his jaw clamped shut.

Trudy took a half step back. She glanced at Ben Garrison and her courage returned.

The detective's eyes focused on her bleeding face. In a voice that could be used to exterminate cockroaches, he said to Watson, "You're under arrest."

"I committed no crime," the man whined. "I'm her patient."

"She says you're not."

"I need your help, Doctor." Watson reached for her but Garrison held him back. "You're ruining my life. My wife said she'd only talk to you."

"Keep quiet," Detective Garrison ordered. "You've got the right to remain silent. I suggest you take that right seriously and shut up."

The man ignored the order. "I didn't do any of those things you're accusing me of. I just need to talk to you, Dr. Jennings."

The man wrenched his head toward Trudy, despite Detective Garrison's hold on him. "I'd never hurt you. I need help to save my marriage. I need you to come with me. My wife said she'd talk to you and nobody else. *She* made me come here to get you."

"You don't get a woman to come with you by assaulting her in a dark parking lot. You've got the right to an attorney. If you cannot afford an attorney one will be..."

"You're *Tru Intervention*," the man went on, despite Garrison's warning. His voice climbed higher because of the arm wrapped around his neck. "You wrote all those books. I've read them all. I know you can help me."

Trudy's hand went to her bleeding cheek. She saw something in the man's eyes. Behind the attack, instead of madness, she saw desperation. She saw sincerity. She'd believed she was being assaulted, but he could have been trying to restrain her just to make her listen. Of course, he had intended to take her with him by force. That was kidnapping. But he just wanted to get her away from here to stage a marriage counseling session. He needed her. This wasn't an attack; it was a cry for help. A clumsy, ill-advised cry for help admittedly, but people did stupid things when they were pushed to the limit.

Detective Garrison held the man with one hand and slipped his cell phone out of his pocket with the other.

*Turn the other cheek. A soft answer turns away wrath.* How had it taken her this long to remember her own advice?

All her life she'd felt a calling to help people. Instead of taking the time to reach out to people in need, she lived in a mansion and wrote perky little best sellers. Her chance to serve those in need had finally come. Instead of hauling the man off to jail, she needed to help him.

"Wait." Trudy held up her hand. "Let him finish."

The detective's eyes cut like blue lasers. "Let him finish attacking you?"

"No," Trudy shrieked and jumped back. Regaining control of herself, she said, "I meant, let him finish what he has to say. Maybe I misunderstood..." She looked behind her at the brick wall, marked with her blood.

"I saw him knock you against that wall hard enough that you'll be bruised in the morning," the detective said. "Your face is bleeding."

Trudy felt the swelling on her upper arms where Watson's crushing grip had locked on her.

"I just wanted to talk to you," Watson insisted. "I've been waiting all night for a chance to ask you questions about how I can get my wife back. I'm sorry I frightened you. I didn't mean..."

"We're out of here." Garrison lifted his phone to eye level.

"Let him finish," Trudy said.

"It's my wife." Watson looked at Garrison's cell phone, and talked fast. "She left me. I've got a problem with my temper. I know that."

"You *think*?" Garrison snorted. He didn't pretend for a second to cover this one up with coughing.

"I've been trying to get control of it. But she wouldn't give me a chance. She left me. I found your book, Dr. Jennings. I read all about your system of intense, personal counseling. I want you to work with my wife and me. I love her. I don't want us to get divorced. With your help, we can start over. We can rediscover the love we've lost."

"You hurt me," Trudy said, uncertain what to do. Being Watson's personal counselor was impossible. She recognized the man's disrespect for women and knew he'd never accept her help.

"I didn't mean to. I've been trying to contact you all summer. Finally, with classes starting up again, I knew you'd be here. I've been waiting for hours. When I saw you, I ran up to you and you jumped and screamed. I...I guess I panicked. I just wanted you to stay and listen. I told you that, but you wouldn't stop fighting me. I shouldn't have held you like that. I didn't mean to be so rough. But I needed you to hear me out."

*He had been talking, and Trudy had been too frightened to listen.* "Do you treat your wife like that when she won't listen to you? If you're putting your hands on her and shoving her into walls, then that's not a bad temper. That's abuse."

Trudy touched her tender cheek again. "If a woman comes away from an encounter with you bleeding, then to blame her fear on the inconveniently placed wall is you trying to deny responsibility.

It's all abuse, and I'd advise her to leave you. Even if she agreed to try and mend the relationship, I'd recommend she do it from a place of safety until you have your anger under control."

"No, I need her. She'd got to come home."

"Mr. Watson, I told you Dr. Pavil will help you, but part of that help will include telling your wife to stay away from you in unsupervised situations for her own protection. She's not safe until the two of you go through counseling and you've made real progress with anger management."

Watson's eyes narrowed. Rage cut deep lines in his face as he struggled to control his breathing. As if it were necessary to force the words past his lips, he said, "That's fine, Doctor. We'll do it your way. I'll do whatever you say."

Trudy noticed he didn't deny abusing his wife.

"We can live apart as long as we're working on our marriage," the man said.

Garrison ignored the exchange. "Let's see some ID." He watched the man with narrow eyes to see if he'd balk at identifying himself.

"Ralph Watson. I live here in Long Pine, on the west side, in the Bourne neighborhood." Watson mentioned the richest part of town as he fumbled in his back pocket for a billfold. Garrison, still holding onto Watson's collar, snagged the wallet and flipped it open.

Trudy could see the man's driver's license behind a cellophane window. His picture looked better than the man in front of her.

Trudy's had several pictures taken by the DMV. They were brutal. It usually took some real doing to look worse than your driver's license.

Garrison glared at Watson. "Are you going to run if I let you go?"

"No." Watson shook his shaggy head. "Running would be an admission of guilt. I had no intention of hurting Dr. Jennings. I will stay here and straighten this out."

Garrison released his grip on Watson's neck. Without taking his eyes off the man, the detective reached into his back pocket and pulled out the handkerchief he'd been coughing into all through class. He handed it to Trudy.

She hesitated as she looked at the cloth.

"Your face is bleeding," Garrison said.

The man looked healthy enough, coughing not-withstanding. "Uh...it's clean."

She took the soft cotton and pressed it to her swollen cheek.

"I'm sorry you were injured, Dr. Jennings," Watson groveled. "I didn't do it. You were trying to get away and you hurt yourself."

Garrison leaned close. "You try and blame her bleeding face on anyone but yourself and you're busted."

Watson held up both hands. "I can see how you thought the worst, Dr. Jennings, and you too, officer. I just didn't think how it would look, me coming at you in the dark that way."

The man paused and sucked in a deep breath. "You can see how stupid I am about women. I'm always doing something wrong." Watson clenched his fists.

Trudy took a step back.

Detective Garrison came to full alert.

"I deserve to be alone. I'm always doing the wrong thing to my wife. I say the wrong thing. I hurt her feelings. And when I try to make it right, it just gets worse." Watson seemed to be planning to beat up on only himself.

Trudy relaxed a little. She didn't think Garrison did.

A week's growth of beard darkened the man's face and accented his blood-shot eyes. He had on a white oxford shirt, sweat-stained and filthy. He'd been so violent. Could he really be here looking for help?

She believed the man probably hadn't come here tonight planning to hurt her. But his out-of-control approach made him dangerous. *Turn the other cheek.* Trudy pulled the handkerchief away from her face. Blood soaked a small area, but the bleeding had stopped. Never had she been given a more clear-cut chance to practice what she preached.

She looked at Watson. "I won't press charges."

"Oh yes, you will," Garrison ordered.

Trudy glanced at him. "No, I won't. That's my decision to make." She turned back to Watson. "But I won't be your counselor. I want you to accept my referral. This doctor will still use my methods."

"No." Watson lurched toward her.

Garrison caught him by the back of the neck. "That's it. We're going downtown."

"Dr. Jennings, I need *your* help. Only you. I've already talked to my wife. She doesn't want to forgive me, but she's read your books and admires your work. She's agreed to try and work on our marriage if you'll counsel us."

"Mr. Watson, I can't possibly be your counselor. For one thing, I have found that men respond better to other men when it comes to anger management."

"Not me. I know you're the right one for me."

"Angry men tend to dismiss a woman's perspective."

"You're wrong."

The fact that he dismissed her perspective wasn't lost on Trudy. "It's part of the psychological profile of someone with anger issues. I've trained many people in my methods and if your wife expressed a willingness to work with me, then that shows she still has hope for the marriage. I'm sure she'd accept another counselor. I'd even be willing to talk with her and explain why another doctor would be better. Now, let me give you Dr. Pavil's number again."

Trudy looked down at the ground and saw her briefcase lying beside her torn up books and papers. It reminded her of how frightened she'd been. She drew in a steadying breath and crouched down to open her briefcase. She sorted through the scattered mess until she found Dr. Pavil's card and rose, handing it to Watson.

"I'll phone him tomorrow and tell him to expect you."

"I don't want him." Watson ignored the card.

"If you are interested in saving your marriage and you think my methods will work, then you'll take the card and phone for an appointment and follow through with everything Dr. Pavil advises. I've worked on the theories, but I'm a teacher. Dr. Pavil has far more clinical experience." She extended the card to Watson.

Scowling, he looked from the card to Trudy.

Garrison swiped the card from Trudy's hand and shoved it into Watson's billfold. "Take the card and get out of here, Watson, before I change my mind about running you in." The detective slapped the wallet against Watson's chest. "She isn't the only one who can press charges. I witnessed the assault. I can do all the pressing myself."

Watson caught the wallet.

He turned his desperate eyes away from Trudy and looked at Garrison. Trudy wasn't in the direct line of fire from the detective's eyes, but she still felt singed.

Watson's Adam's apple bobbed up and down.

Trudy had to dig deep for the courage to reach out and lay her hand on the poor man's quivering shoulder. "Dr. Pavil really can help you better than I, Mr. Watson."

Watson nodded and, with one last look of furious longing at Trudy, he turned and scuttled away into the dark parking lot.

Trudy knees buckled.

The detective caught her before she collapsed.

"You're hurt." He shifted her so his arm was around her waist. "We need to get you to a hospital."

He supported her as he urged her toward a monster black pick-up that stood near the back of the parking lot under a street light.

Trudy let him manhandle her, a testament to how shaken the night had left her.

"That guy is a menace," Detective Garrison said. "You wait. He'll be arrested for something else. He's out of control."

Trudy forced her legs to work. She tried to wriggle loose from Garrison's strong arms, but he wouldn't let go. He seemed determined to bully her into a hospital. He pushed her around almost as much as Watson had, but there was no comparison. His hands were gentle. His voice, though angry about letting Watson go, soothed her with his concern. His clean, alluring, masculine scent calmed her.

Detective Garrison was a nice man.

"That man assaulted you. You gave him a business card and a pep talk. You are a moron."

Nice wasn't the right word.

A hero, with the manners of a pig.

Trudy sighed all the way to her toes. She'd prayed for help and God had sent her Cough Man.

God wasn't kidding when He said He worked in mysterious ways.

"Let me go. Stop it, Cough Man. Quit pushing me around."

Garrison's arm left her waist. Only when she almost fell did she realize how much she'd been leaning on him.

"Koffman? Who's that?" He turned to face her. The warm night breeze of Texas in late August stirred his hair and sent his bangs drooping down his square forehead.

Trudy's eyes widened. "Did I say that out loud?"

"Yes." Garrison ran one hand into his hair, shoving it back. "Who is Koffman? Your husband?"

"I'm not married." Trudy hadn't meant to sound quite so happy to share that news.

"Then who's Koffman?" Detective Garrison waited.

Trudy tried to think of a soft answer, because she thought that might give her a chance to turn away some wrath. Wrath she might be facing if she told the truth about her little nickname for him.

"I'm a policeman. Interrogation is my life." He crossed his arms, looking relentless enough to wait all night. He stared at her and let the silence stretch.

She'd bet he was great at wringing confessions out of people.

She decided to confess herself, anything to get him to go away. "It's you." She smiled. "A little pet name for you. From class."

"Koffman?" A short silence, then Garrison grinned and nodded. "Cough man. Got it."

"Good, maybe I'll put it on the test. You'll need the extra credit points, by the way. I grade heavily on class behavior."

"I'm doomed," Garrison said, not sounding doomed at all.

"Perilously close to doomed, I'm afraid."

"Does saving your life give me a bump in my grade?" He gave her a teasing grin. "That's pretty good behavior."

Trudy felt all the blood drain out of her head. She laid an unsteady hand on Detective Garrison's arm. "What a frightening experience."

She knew Detective Garrison was unhappy with her not pressing charges—figuring that out didn't make her a genius. "I don't think it would have done any good to arrest him. If he told his story like he did to us, the judge would give him the benefit of the doubt. He's probably telling the truth, which doesn't mean he isn't dangerous. I just don't think Watson did anything that he'll get arrested for."

"Maybe you're right," Garrison studied her cheek. "Although your bleeding face would give a judge plenty to think about. No, unless he's made a habit of assaulting women, the only purpose turning him in would have served is documenting his behavior. If he comes at some other woman, he'd have a history of violence and the charges would be taken seriously."

Trudy nodded. "His wife has left him and, to hear him talk, he's not interested in any woman except her. I'll make sure Dr. Pavil knows all this before he starts working with them."

"He's not going to contact Dr. Pavil."

"I'm sure he will."

"Not a chance."

"It's not uncommon to want the doctor who started some new form of therapy, but Dr. Pavil is actually better at working with patients. Mr. Watson will come to understand that."

"You know you're wrong about him not being interested in any woman except his wife." Detective Garrison stared in the direction Watson had gone.

"No, I'm not. His sole motivation is to get her back. What other woman is he interested in?"

Detective Garrison shook his head as if he felt sorry for her. He leaned down close. "He seemed really interested in you."

# CHAPTER THREE

"I'M SORRY." BEN, GENIUS POLICE detective that he was, jerked his hands out of his pockets and caught her as her knees gave out. "I'm so sorry."

He tried to remember another day in his life when he'd apologized this much. *Fifth grade. Daniel Waggoner Middle-School. Six garter snakes in the teacher's lounge.*

"You think he might come back?" Dr. Trudy asked in a voice so weak it made his heart ache. The way she let him bear her weight worried him, too.

Ben hesitated to answer. He'd seen that wild, obsessed expression on Watson's face. He hated to say it but the bald-faced truth was...

"Yeah, I think he might come back."

She sagged more heavily.

Slender, blonde and so lovely it hurt to look at her, Tru came on like a tough little cookie, although he suspected it was a very sweet cookie. Despite her dopey pacifist books, in the classroom, she'd struck him as a lady who stood her ground. At least she acted that way with him. Why had she been so soft on Watson?

"I'm taking you to the hospital." Slinging his arm around her waist, he helped her to his black Ford F-150. The only other vehicle in the parking lot was a silver Cadillac Seville that must belong to teacher lady.

"No, I'm fine." She continued to lean so he ignored her said and kept walking.

Ben had noticed the solid gold in her necklace and earrings and sized up her casual wool slacks, cashmere sweater and Armani blazer, all worn with a complete lack of self-consciousness.

He knew about stuff like this because this kind of property got stolen. He'd never personally known a woman who owned anything like it but he'd smelled money the minute he'd laid eyes on Tru Jennings. Of course, she'd be rich. She'd written half a dozen best-selling pop psychology books. She made regular appearances on Good Morning America. Her first book had been recommended by Oprah, for Pete's sake.

Tru Jennings; celebrity pop psychology flavor of the month, only her flavor had been in style for several years now, ever since her first touchy-feely book about a loving approach to reaching out to sickoes had hit the bestseller list.

She pushed against his chest. When he glanced down and saw a bloodstain on the front of his shirt, he wanted to go after Watson and wreak havoc.

"I don't need a hospital." She sounded weak but determined.

Her gold hoop earrings caught the street light and glittered expensively at him. Pressed against him like this, he could smell her.

She didn't smell like money. She smelled far more alluring than the root of all evil.

Ben hadn't been this close to a woman—unless you counted arresting a bunch of them—since Cara had left him. And—rule of thumb—your average homicide suspect didn't smell that great.

In fact, his job had cost him is fiancé. A women he'd arrested, now out on bail, saw him in a convenience store and came charging at him while Ben stood waiting for Cara to pay for a bottle of water. The crazy woman clawed his face, screaming threats until it made Ben's ears bleed. When he'd tried to restrain her, she'd grabbed a rack off the counter at him and nailed Cara. Then the drugged-out assailant had banged Ben with it hard enough it'd turned his lights out. The woman had run.

The convenience store guy called an ambulance and the cops.

He woke up in the hospital to see Cara standing over him. Five stitches across her chin. The engagement ring she'd been wearing for two weeks, in her hand. Not on her hand. Not anymore.

She'd had dumped him, and she'd been right to do it. Because if danger was a disease then Ben was a carrier. Or at least his job was. Losing soft-hearted Cara had cured him of women and good riddance.

He'd forgotten how soft and sweet-smelling a woman was. Or had he? Maybe Trudy Jennings was just in a soft and sweet-smelling league of her own.

Ben had known all about her cornball philosophy when he'd enrolled in her class. He'd enrolled for one reason only. It was a requirement for his degree. He had to pass her class to graduate. But her passive philosophy wasn't for cops, which meant it wasn't for him.

The Armani, the gold, the Seville, the go-and-sin-no-more way she'd handled her assailant, told him she lived in an ivory tower. Ugliness didn't touch her, and he was glad of that. But it touched him, and he had to be ready for it.

"Are you sure you shouldn't see a doctor?"

"Yes, I'm fine." She stopped touching him, which Ben missed immediately.

"Let me give you a ride home. You may not need the hospital, but you've had yourself a go round. I'm not going to let you drive."

"You're not going to *let* me drive?"

Ben had to fight not to smile. He'd seen her little claws earlier in the classroom. Ben oughta get named as an American diplomat for facing something as laughable as Tru Jennings' simple-minded philosophy and pretend to cough.

He hadn't pulled it off. So, he'd never make it as a diplomat—big surprise. He'd have to get it under control before the next class. But tonight, he hadn't been ready. Between taking down a knife wielding gang member in the morning and enduring the smug, shyster lawyer trying to plead premeditated murder down to a misdemeanor in the afternoon, Ben hadn't been able to contain the laughter.

*Next week, I swear I'll be a good boy.*

"Let   me   tell   you   something,   Mr.   Garrison..."
"Ben." He waited for that to annoy her.

"Mr. Garrison, no one tells me what I can and cannot..."

She hadn't made him wait at all. If fast food restaurants served irritation, Tru would be a world class Unhappy Meal. Deciding *not* to use gentle persuasion, Ben ignored her yammering and tugged his cell phone out of his pocket.

"What are you doing?" Wide-eyed, she looked from the phone to him.

"You're one word away from 911, Tru. If your next words aren't 'yes, Ben, I'd love a ride home,' you'll leave this parking lot in an ambulance."

She crossed her arms. "You don't..."

"That's the word," Ben waggled the phone in her face and, with grand gestures, tapped *nine* into the phone.

She tried to grab it from him. He held it overhead. All her soft-ness tried to fight him for the phone. It was mighty wrong of him to be enjoying this. Which didn't stop him.

"Yes, Ben, I'd love a ride home. C'mon, Tru, say it. You know you're not up to driving."

"Dr. Jennings, to you." She made another grab for the phone. Personally, Ben thought she was wrestling out of her weight class.

"I am your teacher." She seemed pretty strong, grappling for the phone. She probably didn't need a hospital, but he'd seen her eyes lose focus a couple of times. He refused to let her get in that car.

"Strike two, Tru." Ben pressed *one* with great pleasure.

She narrowed her eyes. He made a production of reaching for the *one* again.

"Yes, Ben." She jammed her hands on her hips and parroted his words. "I'd love a ride home."

He deleted the call and dropped his phone back into his pocket. "Smart girl. You didn't get that Doctor tacked onto your name at *Clown* College, after all."

"Mr. Garrison..."

"Call me Ben."

"*Mr. Garrison...*"

Ben pulled out his phone again. "You know this could be fun. I could tease you like this all night and never get tired of it."

Tru sank her face into her hands. Ben stepped close. "Are you all right? Maybe you really *do* need an ambulance."

She shook her head, uncovered her face and lifted her chin. "Let's get going. I've got a long day tomorrow and I need some rest."

Unlocking his truck with the remote on his key chain, he opened the door for her. He looked from her five foot seven body to his massive truck frame. "Need a boost?"

"No." She glared at him, then wobbled just a little.

Ben wrapped his arm around her, all humor gone. "Turn around."

She obeyed, which worried him. Putting his hands on her slender waist, he lifted her into the truck, careful not to bump her head. Experienced in emergencies, he took careful note of her scraped face and trembling hands. He studied her pupils and her messed up hair.

"Are you sure you're all right?" He hovered just inches from her, her blue eyes so vulnerable. "I let you talk me out of the emergency room, but maybe you have a concussion."

She shook her head. "It's just reaction. I'm on adrenaline overload or something."

Ben pulled a flashlight out of his glove compartment and shined it in her eyes.

"Stop." She swatted at the glaring light.

"Settle down." Holding her chin, he watched her pupils contract. "Is there anyone at home? I'm not going to leave you there alone. I can stay, or I can call a police woman for you."

"I've got a housekeeper who stays until I get home, and that includes when I work late on Monday night. She doesn't like me coming into an empty house. She'll stay all night if I ask her."

"Call her so she can make arrangements." Ben produced his cell phone.

"I have my own phone." Trudy looked at her hands, then looked back at Ben. She turned toward the building she'd just had her head slammed into.

Ben's eyes landed on all the stuff she'd dropped by the Psycho Building.

"It's over there by the Psych building." She pointed.

He took a minute to get into his first aid kit and crush up an instant ice pack and rest it on her face.

"Thanks." She took over holding it while he buckled her seat belt. Then he got in and wheeled the truck up to the building. He hopped out, gathered her things, rested them on the console between them and set off. By the time he'd driven her home, he'd know for ure if she was all right.

She gave him directions to Cullen Heights, a ritzy lakeside neighborhood right on the edge of the prosperous Texas town. Only a few miles from the university, arguably the most elegant neighborhood in a wealthy city—maybe one notch below where Watson lived.

It was a long way from where he lived and that had to do with a lot more than geography.

He listened as she phoned her housekeeper and asked her to spend the night without explaining why.

"You'd better warn her about what happened. If this guy comes after you again, your housekeeper needs to be alert."

Tru had already ended the call. "Eleanor fusses over me too much as it is. That's why she always stays until she's sure I'm home safe. She worries that I could be gone all night before anyone missed me."

"Sounds like a lady who cares about you." Ben was glad Tru had someone like that. He also noticed she didn't mention a boyfriend who could check on her.

Silence.

Afraid she'd read his mind—or maybe afraid he'd read his own mind—he changed the subject. "Look, I want to apologize again for uh... coughing during the class."

"Laughing, you mean." She had a sharp, classy little northern accent. She'd been slow about getting to the great state of Texas.

Ben sighed. He'd been hoping for another polite, if insincere, acceptance of his apology. Wasn't that the right thing to do according to her own philosophy?

More talk seemed like a bad idea but he thought of Watson coming at her in the dark and knew this was his chance to talk some sense into her. "It's just that it doesn't work, Tru. I mean, it might work when problems are less severe, like in a counselor's office, but on the street...well, cops can't just stand there and let the bad guys shoot. We've got to fight back. We're not just defending ourselves, we're protecting others. Your methods have nothing to do with police work. They might work in personal relationships, but they've got nuthin' to do with the world I live in. And no soft answer tonight, to Watson, was going to get him to back off."

"My theories are about right and wrong. There's no career that absolves you, Ben."

She'd used his name, without being threatened with an ambulance. *It's just stupid to like that so much.*

"So you're sayin' I should turn the other cheek to some meth head, who's unloading a gun at me? That can't be right."

Tru turned to him. He glanced over. Her right cheek, raw and bloody, shone in the headlights of on-coming traffic. She'd low-ered the ice pack, noticed, and returned it to her cheek. In the other hand she clenched his blood-stained handkerchief.

"I can't tell you what to do. You save people's lives by taking hard measures when a violent criminal is on a rampage. But I don't think right and wrong can have a label with a bunch of bureau-cratic legalese full of subsections and exceptions to the rules."

Ben turned off the quiet street leading away from the university and got on a four lane. The traffic was light this time of night. "Sitting out there in your classroom, I kept picturing myself sweet talking the gang banger I busted today into handing over his knife and turning himself in." Ben shrugged. "It just made me laugh."

Merging, he headed north toward Cullen Heights. "I read your book in preparation for the class. It's idealism, which is wonder-ful...for you. But tonight, I couldn't distance myself from the unrealistic way you look at the world."

"You read my book?" Tru asked.

"Yep." He hoped that earned him some brownie points because he needed them to pass and he needed to pass to earn his bach-elor's degree. If they gave credits for life experience, he'd have a doctorate by now.

"So, you're the one."

Ben glanced over at her.

She smiled at him.

He smiled back. They'd sold millions of copies.

"Is it easy to put what you believe in a box like that during work hours?" Tru faced forward.

"A box?"

"Yes." Tru stacked her books more neatly between them, then shifted them onto her lap. Every move graceful, her voice was so kind and gentle it was enchanting, almost like being under her spell.

"You're kind and respond to evil with good when it's easy, but don't bother when it's hard."

Well, that broke the spell.

"I don't do that." He focused on wringing the steering wheel's neck. "I'm a good person at work and at home. I never flirt with gray areas of the law. I never use unnecessary force." Much. "I go to church on Sunday."

Tru faced him. "I believe you."

He almost pulled over. They were getting close to her home and he wanted to finish this. He had something to prove to this naïve little woman. He might have done it if they hadn't been traveling sixty-five miles an hour. "Well, good."

She inhaled deeply, no doubt gathering her strength to yell at him. "Turning the other cheek is just simple wisdom." She spoke just above a whisper.

"You're using that 'a soft answer turneth away wrath' voice on me, aren't you?" Ben turned onto Broadway and headed east.

Tru laughed. "Caught that did you?"

"Yep."

"Did it work? Has your wrath been turneth'ed away?"

Ben glanced at her pretty smile and rolled his eyes. He looked back at the street and shrugged. "Some. I wasn't all that wrathful to begin with…not at you."

"I guess you weren't." Tru patted him on the arm with her soft callus-free hand. "I should save it for when you're really a grouch."

"So, tell me how I translate your idealism into my job? In a perfect world, you're right, but then in a perfect world, everyone would be kind and gentle in the face of anger and if everyone was, then there wouldn't be any anger, so the whole exercise would be unnecessary. If I follow what you say, does that mean I can't be a cop? Because I can't do my job if I turn the other cheek. A soft answer pegs you as a weak link, and the bad guys turn their guns on you first."

Tru didn't say anything. Ben took that as an admission that he was right—which he was.

"Admit it, Tru, the only way to agree with you is to say that, between fighting a war and being a cop, the last twelve years of my life have been a mistake. And if I stay in my job, the rest of my life will be a mistake, too." He looked at her, then shook his head. Trudy Jennings didn't have the wisdom of the ages at her dainty polished fingertips.

He realized he'd been hoping for a lot more out of Tru's class than three credit hours and a college diploma. He knew he'd got-ten too cynical at work. He knew he'd been battered by dealing with the underbelly of Long Pine. It was a prosperous town but like any city it had its bad side.

"Your idealistic theories only work if I'm willing to die for them. I'm not going to die so a criminal can run rampant, killing others. If I live like you advise in your books, I'll be dead by the weekend."

"I'm right Ben, and if you try it you can find a way," Tru said in that confounded soft voice. "That's the best I can tell you."

It was an out for her. Ben understood that. But she had a lot of nerve challenging his whole life with no idea what he should do to fix it.

He followed her directions home. She told him her gate code and they drove into an elegant stucco house in the heart of Long Pine's old money neighborhood. It looked like a Mexican Hacienda on All-American steroids with three floors of pink stucco, a porch with stucco arches across the front and a red tile roof.

"Those books must sell pretty well, huh?"

"Like hotcakes, pal." She tilted her head and gave him a sassy smile.

Ben had to admit that, naïve as she was in her teaching, up until now, he'd been thinking about her with less than student—teacher appropriate thoughts. He'd also been thinking about her with less than cop—victim appropriate thought. She was just too pretty and sweet to think about without a few inappropriate thoughts.

But those thoughts shriveled up and died when he saw her pink mansion. He drove up to the front door, lit up like an operating room at high noon.

He climbed out of his truck and felt like he'd landed in Oz. He needed to knock his ruby slippers together and get out of here.

# CHAPTER FOUR

OPENING HER DOOR, HE UNLATCHED her seatbelt and eased her to the ground. She moaned as she slid down.

The sound made him forget all about escaping. "You're hurt worse than you admitted."

"Just stiff. It's nothing." She let him settle his arm around her waist and guide her toward the house.

The door swung open before they reached the four stone steps that led up to the porch.

"Land sakes, child, what happened to you?" A Sherman tank with a short mop of gray curls stormed out to meet them. Ben moved out of the way when the woman slid her plump hand around Tru's middle. He was certain the tank would have no qualms about leaving waffle tracks on him otherwise.

"I'm okay, Eleanor. A little bruised, but nothing serious." Tru leaned against the woman, but Ben could tell Tru bore her own weight.

He let her go but stayed close to catch her if need be.

"You're hair's all mussed." The housekeeper brushed the hair back with utmost gentleness. Her voice rose in alarm. "What happened to your face?"

"I...I..." Tru's voice broke.

Ben moved up beside them. "I'm a policeman, ma'am. A man frightened her. She decided her injuries weren't serious enough to warrant a trip to the Emergency Room, but I'm worried about her. I'm glad you'll be with her tonight. She shouldn't be alone after a trauma like this."

"Ben." Tru lifted her head and blazed a look at him. "I told you we weren't going to tell her what happened."

"And I disagreed with you, Tru-Blue. I'm telling Eleanor every-thing. If that guy wants in here, Eleanor needs to be on guard."

Ben tried to picture Eleanor on guard, but the image just wouldn't come into focus. Then he pictured her guarding a plate of chocolate chip cookies from a hungry little boy. That developed right away. He substituted Tru's life for cookies and he had himself a bodyguard.

"Tru-Blue?" Eleanor asked, arching one gray eyebrow at Ben.

"She'll just worry." Tru let go of Eleanor and walked into the house ahead of both of them.

Ben noticed the etched glass front door and wondered how tough the glass was. Not his idea of security. He stepped into a three-story foyer just behind Eleanor and tried his best to breathe the rarified air.

Eleanor caught up to Tru and supported her again. Ben flanked Tru on the other side, their feet clicking on the marble tiles. An open stairway curved up on their right and several doors stretched down a wide hall on their left.

"That's the whole idea. She *should* worry." He leaned forward and talked across Tru. "Don't you want to worry, Eleanor?"

Eleanor smiled at him. He thought she might look the other way at cookie-snitching time, but not when it came to defending Tru. "I absolutely love nothing better than worrying."

"That's a fact," Tru said with a glum shake of her head. She lifted her hand to her cheek.

"Do you have aspirin or something, Eleanor? Tru has a head-ache."

"He calls you Tru-Blue?" Eleanor asked. "And you're okay with that?"

"How do you know I have a headache?" Tru turned her narrow eyes at him and shot him with a quiver full of blue arrows. "I hav-en't complained."

"You got smacked in the side of the head and you're bleeding. I guessed."

Eleanor frowned at her boss. "I'll be back in a minute with something to clean up that scrape and some ibuprofen."

"This ice bag isn't cold anymore, can you bring more?" Ben asked.

"Yes." Eleanor studied Tru, frowning. "Are you hurt anywhere else?"

"I'm fine. Just shaken up."

"Would you answer the same if the policeman weren't here? I can toss him out if you want."

"Good luck with that." Ben grinned at Eleanor as he imagined the stout little lady ejecting him. He didn't underestimate her.

Eleanor shook her head. "I don't think it'll be necessary. Take her through there and get her settled." She pointed at the third door on the left, then nailed Tru with a scowl. "And when I get back, you two are telling me everything."

Eleanor steamrolled down the hall in a huff.

Ben guided Tru into a room that was bigger than his house, although if he included his tiny fenced yard, he thought he had her beat.

"We'll tell her everything except why you're calling me by that ridiculous nickname." Tru sank onto the couch.

"It just rolls off the tongue. Your idealistic books, the classes you teach at Bella Vista, your kind treatment of everyone..." Ben paused for a moment. "...except me. Your bruised, bleeding cheek from where you turned it. You are Tru-Blue. You put your money where your mouth is, Doc, which is dumb but honorable. I admire that."

"You admire that I'm dumb?"

"I didn't say that, exactly," Ben protested, pretty sure he'd said exactly that. And he wasn't going to take it back neither. Not until Tru toughened up.

Eleanor bustled in, pills and a bottle of Evian in one hand and a small first aid kit in the other. She handed the medicine to Tru while she broke the seal on the bottle of water.

Ben watched Tru read the medicine bottle, shake her head, and set the small container on a side table.

"No, Eleanor, not these."

"They'll help. Take them just this once."

Ben had a vision of a domineering, Svengali-like housekeeper, feeding drugs to poor little Dr. Jennings. Eleanor didn't look the part but, as a cop, suspicion came naturally to him. Or maybe he was just a snoop.

"No, I don't want to start that."

"This isn't *starting* anything. It's late. You're hurt. This will help."

He picked up the bottle of pills.

"Hey." She grabbed for the bottle. Ben had pleasant visions of her wrestling with him again. He held onto the pills.

"Ibuprofen P.M.?" He pried open the lid. The tablets inside were what the label said they were. He looked between Eleanor and Tru. "Not exactly crack cocaine, so what's the problem?"

"I have a little problem with insomnia." Tru said as if it hurt to admit it.

"And these help?" Ben asked.

"Not really." She snagged the bottle back while he was distracted. Eleanor wet a fluffy white wash cloth with Evian and gently dabbed Tru's battered face. "They might. You've never tried them."

"So the rich wash their cuts and scrapes with Evian." He winced every time the housekeeper touched the wound.

Tru glared at him.

As she fussed over Tru, Eleanor added, "Give them a chance tonight. It's late and you're tired. You've had a shock. If you get wound up from this, like you do sometimes in the night, you might never get to sleep."

"I don't want to depend on medication. It worries me."

"It's not habit forming." Eleanor soothed some antibiotic cream on Tru's scrapes. "It says so right on the bottle. I think there are laws that say they can't lie about those things."

"How can it not be habit forming? If it works, I'll need them every night. That's a habit."

"It's not like you'll go into withdrawal if you quit taking them. You'll just lay awake—just like you do now. How would you ever know you'd become dependent?" Eleanor clucked as she frowned over Tru's cheek.

"It's a crutch." Tru's pout came close to resembling a petulant two-year-old. Ben bit back a grin.

"I promise I'll drive you to the Betty Ford clinic myself if there's trouble." Eleanor studied Tru's wound with an intensity worthy of an ER nurse. "Give them a chance."

"Take the pills, Tru-Blue." Ben handed her the water. "You can always go on the wagon tomorrow. For now, it'll take some of the swelling out of your cheek."

Eleanor pulled out her own instant ice bag, crushed it between her hands, wrapped it in a small towel, then pressed it gently to

Tru's cheek. Tru held it. Eleanor backed up and seemed satisfied with her nursing. She sniffed at Tru and gave Ben a 'thank you' smile. "I have some decaf coffee in the kitchen, Mr...?"

"Detective. Ben Garrison. I'm a homicide detective with Long Pine PD."

"Homicide." Eleanor's hand went to her throat.

"He's a student in my class, Eleanor. There is no homicide in any way connected with this mess. I got pushed around a little by a man after class..."

"A lunatic shoved her against the Psycho building." Ben gave Tru his best gun-slinger look.

She didn't flinch. "The man caught my arm to get my attention."

"He tried to kidnap her," Ben added.

"He begged me to go with him," Tru insisted.

"He grabbed her hair and ripped out a handful." Ben pushed Tru's disheveled hair back from the scrape on her cheek.

She jerked her head away and grimaced. "He tried to make me listen to him."

"He smacked her face against a brick building..." Ben turned to Eleanor.

"I misunderstood his intentions." Tru caught her housekeeper's arm. "I struggled and injured myself in the course of trying to get away."

"*Injured yourself?*" Ben shouted. He fought to remain calm. "He was going to take her with him, who knows where."

Eleanor gasped.

"We weren't going to upset her, Ben." Tru dumped two pills into her hand and swallowed them like she was a starving African villager.

Ben wondered how bad her head hurt. He regretted that he was probably making it worse. "We were absolutely going to upset her. I distinctly remember deciding to upset her."

"No, you were going to worry me." Eleanor looked upset and worried. "But upsetting me is fine, too. Go ahead, Detective Garrison."

"It's Ben."

Eleanor nodded.

"Psycho Building?" Tru asked. She drank a few delicate sips of the Evian. "You mean the Psych Building?"

Ben ignored her. He hadn't meant to use his private nickname for the Gehring Building. Of course, she'd slipped up with Koffman, so he owed her.

"After I dragged him off of Tru, the man claimed he wanted her help to reconcile with his wife. He'd approached her before, and he wasn't satisfied when she referred him to another doctor. He admitted he was abusive."

"Dragged him off of her?" Eleanor rested her hand on Tru's shoulder. "Trudy, I want to hear every word, right now."

"You've already heard every word, plus a bunch of stuff Ben is making up."

"It's true and you know it."

"He didn't admit to abusing his wife."

"He didn't deny it when you accused him of it." Ben looked at Eleanor. "That's the kind of thing I'd deny in a heartbeat if someone accused me of doing it. Tru refused to work with him and offered him a colleague's name."

"Poor Dr. Pavil," Eleanor said. "You do keep that man busy."

Tru sank against the back of the couch. Ben was on his feet, ready to scoop her up and head for the hospital.

"Knock it off." She waved him back. "I'm just tired."

"Maybe the pills are kicking in already. I'd better go. I'll run Watson's name through NCIC, to see if he has a criminal history."

"Leave the poor man alone. Let Dr. Pavil help him."

*Watson was beyond help and anyone with half a brain could see that.* Ben shook his head. *An idealist. Nothing more annoying.* "You'll check on her every two hours, all night, Eleanor?"

"I don't expect you to stay up all night watching me," Tru insisted.

"Every two hours," Eleanor said. "Done."

"I don't think she has a concussion, but she took quite a hit, so we'd better be on the safe side."

"Don't talk about me as if I'm not here."

"If you can't wake her," Ben told Eleanor, "call an ambulance."

"There will be no 911 calls from this house for a scratch." Trudy insisted.

"An ambulance," Eleanor listened with the kind of concentration most people reserved for memorizing scripture. "Absolutely."

Ben smiled down at Tru.

She glared up at him. "You're obsessed with ambulances."

Ben jerked his shoulder in a tiny shrug. "I've been accused of worse. What time do you have to be at the college in the morning?"

"Nine." She tried to sit up.

Ben knew he had to leave. She needed rest. *Insomnia?* He hoped she could sleep. "I'll be here at eight-thirty."

"Why?" She sat straighter, her eyes narrowed.

"You need a ride to work."

"I'll call a taxi." She stood and braced herself against the couch's overstuffed arm.

Ben studied her and decided she was handling herself all right. "I'll be here at eight-thirty. I'm not letting you ride in a taxi until I've run a check on this nut case."

"He is not a nut case."

"I'm the reason—," he cut her off. "You don't have your car. Indulge me. I need to talk to campus security anyway."

"What about?"

"And you're not to be alone in that building late at night." He headed toward the door, hoping to escape before she could say...

"I'll get to work myself, Detective Garrison."

"Eleanor, have her ready. I'm a busy man." Ben grabbed the handle of the frivolous, unsafe door and hustled to escape before he could be privy to any more of Tru's stubborn ideas about how she should conduct her life.

He jogged down her four perfect stone steps. He wheeled his black truck around her perfectly circular driveway, and headed toward her wrought iron fence. It magically opened for him. Or maybe Eleanor pushed a button in the house. Either way, it was all perfect. Too perfect.

On his way home, he swung into a Wal-Mart and walked around until he remembered how real people lived.

He pushed a shopping cart, hunting for pork rinds and generic shampoo as he mulled over what was so fascinating about Tru Jennings.

Sure, she was pretty—a special kind of pretty that tapped into all his protective instincts.

Sure, she smelled great. It lured him, made him want to be close to her so he could smell her again.

Sure, she was vulnerable and that called out to him. He was a cop, and she was in danger.

She was an optimist, and had awakened the idealist in him that he'd buried long ago. He'd joined the force to serve and protect, to fight for truth, justice, and the American Way.

No, wait...that was why he'd wanted to be Superman when he was six.

When he'd joined the force, he'd wanted to save every troubled person he met. The years had passed and he'd grown up and exchanged idealism for common sense. He'd figured it was a trade up.

Tru had a long way to go.

If there was a balance scale functioning in his head, Tru would come out as a lost cause.

TSTL. Too Stupid To Love.

# CHAPTER FIVE

T<sup>STL</sup>
   Trudy lay awake and fumed. *That over-bearing Detective Ben Koffman.*

*Too Stupid To Live.*

She tried to put him out of her mind by staring at the Monet prints on her bedroom wall. She'd decorated the wall for sleepless nights like this, with a low wattage light within easy reach that shined on the delicate watercolor impressions of garden flowers.

A floral cloth that matched the Monet draped the huge bedroom window that showcased a spectacular view. Straw flower wreaths bursting with soft pastels and rough earthy texture brought out the same gentle colors.

It was only for her. Only to please her burning eyes when they would not close.

She did deep breathing exercises and prayed. No closer to sleep, she opened the window to invite the night breeze, to lull her to sleep.

But tonight, the sights and sounds did nothing to soothe or entice sleep to overtake her.

So, she played her word games and when her mind wandered from them, she outlined chapters for future books. This usually worked, but not tonight.

Memories of Watson's savage grip on her arms and his rabid hysteria twisted her stomach. Common sense told her she'd made a mistake not pressing charges. Ben was right: at least there would have been a record of his abuse. If something else happened, the police would look closer.

Trudy shuddered when she imagined 'something else.'

Twice, she decided to tell Ben she'd changed her mind about pressing charges. Twice, she heard Watson's sincere regret and decided to forget the whole thing.

Or she would have, but for the nagging fear that he'd be back.

Trudy pushed back the covers and got up. She felt fuzzy from the sleep aid she'd taken. Instead of putting her to sleep, it merely made her stupid.

So, she decided it was the perfect night to start her new book on bullies.

What better condition to be in to write about bullies than when she was loopy on pain and sleep medication, and in pain from being pushed around by one?

*Tru Intervention: Bullies.*

She could hear the screams now from the psychiatric community. But she could also hear the applause from the common folks. It was her knack for throwing conventional wisdom out the window and replacing it with a Christian approach, cloaked in psychological terms, that had catapulted her modest works into bestsellers.

Trudy wanted to apply her pacifist philosophy to children who were bullies. Many of them acted out the lack of love they received at home. She hoped her turn-the-other-cheek ideas would change hearts all across the school yards of America. But before her ideas did that, there would be the usual screams of protest.

Trudy smiled as she imagined the indignation among psychiatrists, most of whom preferred a mental health label, medication, and years of talk therapy, which guaranteed a six-figure income.

She walked to the laptop on the desk in her bedroom and tapped the keypad. The black screen dissolved into bright blue. She left the room lights off, except for the spotlight on her Monets. The darkness gave her a feeling of intimacy with her subject. She could write her private thoughts into the book, her beliefs in the perfect truth of the Bible, her dreams of a loving world.

Writing energized her. Once started, she'd face at least another two hours of sleeplessness, which meant a three o'clock bedtime.

She'd been tired before; she'd be tired again. She needed to write a book about how overrated sleep was.

Of course, she'd been thinking that for years, but she was always too tired to write it.

Before she opened the new file for the book, she checked her e-mail. She deleted the Viagra ads, the offers to see famous people naked, and the second mortgage pitches.

Next, she read her fan mail. Most of it convinced her she was doing the right thing. She touched the screen as she read one poignant letter that talked about her book planting seeds that had blossomed into a brand new faith in Jesus Christ. Letters like this made everything—the critics, the sleepless nights, the pressure of fame—worthwhile.

A chill ran up her spine when she saw the subject line of the next e-mail: *Give me what I want.*

She quickly deleted it. The next one popped open when the one she deleted disappeared.

*"Give me what I want, or I'll take it."*

She'd been deleting the same e-mail for a month. She got her share of fruitcakes, no big deal. But she'd received letters saying the same cryptic sentence, and had told her personal assistant Liz to toss them. As she deleted the e-mails without opening them, her skin prickled and bumps rose on her arms. It sounded familiar.

She closed her eyes. She could see Watson's face, pressed close to hers. She could smell his breath, hear his whispered words in her ear: *'Give me what I want, or I'll take it.'*

Had he said those exact words?

The darkened room had been serene a moment ago, now danger lurked in its dark corners. The soft wreaths on the wall transformed into huge eyes watching her. The draped fabric on her windows, her closet, her ruffled bed skirt, all became hiding places.

Trudy trembled deep inside at the memory of those terrifying moments with Watson.

She should have let Ben call the police.

No, Watson was distraught, desperate. He needed her help. All the damage had been caused by her struggles against him.

Her hand strayed to her arms. She could feel the welts from his crushing fingers. She looked at the menacing e-mail.

Was her advice naïve? Did only a fool not fear evil? *Did only a fool turn the other cheek?* In the sinister gloom, Trudy decided God could warn of danger. To ignore fear was an act of unfaithfulness.

"I'll ask Ben about it tomorrow." She printed out the e-mail.

She replied to the people who talked about the changes in their lives since they'd read her book. By the time she finished, she'd shaken off the fear of those odd e-mails.

Then she spent a long time in prayer. Centered in her faith and sure of her message, she began to type, secure in her belief that God would approve.

"I guess I don't have to worry about whether I can wake you."

Trudy jumped and squealed. She smacked her knee on the underside of her computer desk and whirled around to face... Eleanor.

Eleanor shook her gray head and frowned. "You might be able to get by with four hours of sleep, but don't you think you should rest tonight, considering you were beaten up in a parking lot?"

Trudy glanced behind her at the clock on her computer. She looked back with a grimace. "I lost track of the time."

Distant thunder rolled. She'd been writing for two hours, and her head brimmed with ideas. The writing exhilarated her more than usual.

"Liz will be here before you leave in the morning."

Trudy thought of the woman she'd hired as her personal assistant six months ago. "Eleanor, that's just mean."

Eleanor smirked, a gleam in her eye. "She's going to see that you're exhausted, and she won't be pleased. And you know what she's like when she's not pleased."

"Don't act like you agree with her, El. I know you can't stand her." Trudy didn't want to go into how much she regretted hiring Liz.

Eleanor shrugged. "Even a stopped clock is right twice a day. In this, Liz would be right."

"I'm done for the night." Trudy gave Eleanor her most sincere smile. "I'm glad you interrupted me. I got lost in the work."

Eleanor's oh-right look told her she was unimpressed with Trudy's acting. "Whose ox are you going to gore this time, sweetie?" Eleanor leaned forward and studied the laptop screen.

"The usual. Almost everybody's."

Eleanor's eyes moved to the scrape on Trudy's cheek. Like a good girl, Trudy endured the inspection, enjoying Eleanor's loving concern.

Meeting anger with gentleness and turning the other cheek were Trudy's talking points, but she was so sheltered, she seldom got the chance to actually do them. She didn't know first hand if her ideas worked, except, of course, for the grateful e-mails and letters from people she'd helped.

There was no time to commission a scientific poll tonight. "I'm going to bed, I promise."

Eleanor's eyebrows lifted.

"I'll save my work and shut down for the night. Even if I can't sleep, I can rest, right?" She said the last part before Eleanor said it to her. It was one of Eleanor's favorite maternal platitudes.

"Besides, it's going to storm soon. I have to shut the computer off to protect it from power surges."

"I'm waiting here until that beast is off. I'm tempted to confiscate it." Eleanor crossed her arms and planted her feet. She was a sweetheart, but some of Trudy's bully book might be suited for the little tyrant.

Trudy narrowed her eyes and tried to look as if she were boss.

"But I'll leave the computer and settle for a promise."

Trudy was beaten. "I promise." She always kept her promises, and Eleanor knew it. Turning, Trudy realized she'd written fifty pages of her book in a single night. She shut down tomorrow's bestseller with a smug grin.

"Good night then, my girl." Eleanor left.

Trudy walked to the window. Lightning lit up the quiet beach. The approaching fall had begun to cool the night air. She cranked the window shut. The rolling hills glowed like a black jewel as the sky flared with light. Her backyard opened onto the beach of a small lake surrounded by multi-million dollar homes like hers. She owned her own private stretch of it.

As the storm tossed surf of the lake rolled in to shore, a bolt of lightning split the sky and a dark form standing on the beach moved to avoid the incoming water.

Jumping away from the window, her heart pounding, Trudy leaned against the wall beside the window. He'd seen her. He couldn't have helped it. The window crank rattled and hers was certain to be the only light on in the long strip of old mansions along the beach.

She dropped to the floor, her skin crawling. It had to be Watson. She scrambled on her hands and knees to her bed and hit the lights, plunging her room into darkness broken only by lightning.

Trembling, she climbed into bed and pulled the covers up to her chin. Eleanor was ruthless about locking the house up tight. Trudy's window was on the second floor with no way up.

She willed her heart to stop hammering. *Use your head, for heaven's sake. It could have been anybody. It could be another insomniac neighbor.*

She didn't think so. Wide-eyed, she stared at the darkened walls where her Monets roosted. The night stretched endlessly before her.

She tried to settle herself down by playing mind games. They didn't help, but they kept her from going completely crazy.

Genesis

Exodus

Leviticus

Numbers

Deuteronomy

Joshua

Judges

Her bedside clock clicked over to three a.m. and there was no sleep in sight.

Ruth

I Samuel

II Samuel

I Kings

II Kings...

# CHAPTER SIX

BEN DROVE UP TO THE gate and wondered if Tru had meant for him to let himself in. He punched in the front gate code, curious about what kind of security she had.

Driving up the majestic curved driveway to the pink mansion, he enjoyed the cool Long Pine morning, the air washed clean by last night's rain. He wondered, too, if she was even out of bed yet. He'd left after eleven, after all.

He parked, hopped out, and walked to the front door. Testing things further, he turned the knob and discovered the door wasn't locked. Jaw clenched in irritation at the reckless behavior of a sup-posedly smart woman, he slipped inside.

"Tell me you lock your doors at night, Tru-Blue," he muttered as he snapped the lock and turned to the foyer, talking to the cascad-ing chandelier showering him with light from a couple hundred tiny bulbs.

"No one is that careless in this day and age, right?"

He walked in the direction Eleanor had gone last night to get medicine and bandages. Maybe he'd find faithful Eleanor in the kitchen, wrapped in protective padding, tossing raw meat to the killer Dobermans—which would come out to attack him just as soon as they'd been fed. That would explain everything and he'd be forced to rethink his looming decision that Tru was an idiot.

He entered the kitchen.

No Eleanor. No dogs.

Great smelling coffee, though.

He took the time to search the huge kitchen for mugs and poured himself a cup. The steaming pot told him that *somebody* lived here.

"Just how much are you going to let me yell at you, Tru, and still turn the other cheek?" Ben muttered as he wandered the house, fighting his rising temper. Sure, she was naïve, but maybe she'd never dealt with stalkers and crazed assailants, before. Or cops.

Tru might be one of the lucky people who had never been touched by ugliness. She still wore rose-colored glasses and wrote sweet little books, didn't she? Maybe there was a scant possibility that with normal people, her theories might occasionally work.

As he went back to the front entrance, peeking behind every door on the way, he asked God to forgive him for his methods. "I'm not going to baby her. I'm going to push her and push her until she wises up, God. I'm going to test her limits."

He stood at the bottom of the stairs and yelled, "Does anybody live here?"

Nothing answered him except the echo of his own voice in the cavernous entryway. Where was she? Had the assailant from last night come back?

Before he could panic, he heard water running. He glanced at his watch. *If she's just now taking a shower, I'm going to be late and she's going to be sorry.*

The front door behind him swung open. He turned, bracing for an attack, expecting to see the assailant from the parking lot last night.

But a middle-aged woman with a key to the front door walked in, sucking hard on a cigarette. She tossed it, leaving it glowing on the front step, and shut the door. "Who're you?"

"I was here first. Who're you?" Ben waited.

"But I belong here and you don't." She reminded him of a bumblebee, with her yellow-and-black-striped sweater on a short, circular body. Her pasty-white face was lined with smoker's wrinkles. Her short, black, spiky hair spewed from gray roots, and bore an unfortunate resemblance to antennae. She marched toward him as if she intended to attack, but Ben had studied human nature and he suspected she was more the type to talk someone to death.

He assumed the cop stance, legs spread, arms crossed. "I'm a friend of Tru's."

The bumblebee continued advancing. Ben almost took a step back. The woman seemed to be boring into his brain with her angry eyes.

"I know Trudy's friends." When she frowned, her entire face deepened into wrinkles that would make a bulldog jealous, wrinkles that had eroded into her face from a lifetime of scowling. "You're not one of them. And no one calls her Tru, which means you're *not* her friend. So, I repeat, who are you?"

"I call her Tru. And I'm a new friend. Your turn." Ben wondered if the woman would be interested in working for the police department, scaring criminals into confessing. Fear was a commodity with cops, and this woman had cornered the market.

After a few seconds of high-powered glaring, the woman turned away from Ben and shouted upstairs. "Trudy, you get down here right now!"

Ben would have obeyed her in a heartbeat. A gargantuan bumblebee slash bulldog mix, with all the worst qualities of both. *Genetic engineering gone horribly awry.*

Trudy appeared at the top of the stairs, dressed in a black turtleneck sweater, black slacks and a maroon blazer. Her sleek blonde hair pulled back in another tidy barrette at the base of her neck. She carried black heels by little straps. "Liz, you're here. Good."

*Good?* Ben didn't think there was anywhere, not even some parallel universe, where the presence of a cranky, three-hundred-pound bumblebee in an entryway could be considered *good*.

Tru nearly fell over her feet rushing down the stairs as if she were a naughty child, afraid to face her angry mother, but more afraid not to.

"What's he doing here?" Liz strode over to Tru and grabbed her chin. "And what happened to your cheek? We've got a photo shoot coming up."

"When?" Tru allowed the woman to twist her face left and right as the bumblebee studied her from every angle. "What photo shoot?"

"There's always a photo shoot. Just plan on it and don't get yourself beat up. How are we supposed to cover these bruises?"

Ben clenched his fingers into fists to keep from pulling the woman off Tru.

"Don't worry, Liz. I'm sure make-up will cover it."

Ben flinched when he listened to Tru take the cranky old bat's criticism and try to calm her down with excuses. If the old bat had touched him like that, she'd be lucky to get all of her fingers back.

"Really, Liz, it's not deep. We'll just—"

"Did you do something that will bring us bad publicity? You have an image to maintain. Barroom brawls wreak havoc on sales."

"No, I didn't do anything that—"

"Give me a straight answer right now, Trudy, or I'll call the police."

Tru shook her head with wide-eyed fear. "No, Liz, don't do that. He *is* the police."

Ben thought he was a little more than that, what with saving her life last night and being her personal bodyguard today, but he'd take that up with Tru in private.

Bumblebee turned on Ben, he could almost imagine a stinger quivering. "Why do we need the police?"

Ben waited for Tru to defend him, tell this old bat how he'd saved her.

"We don't need the police for anything, Liz. He's a student in one of my classes."

Liz sneered. "Been left back a couple dozen times, pal?"

Glowering, Ben opened his mouth.

"He's giving me a ride to the campus today."

"Why?" Liz gave him one last glare, then refocused her laser eyes on Tru as if she were planning to perform brain surgery. Liz crossed her arms across her rotund belly and tapped her foot.

Tru's jaw dropped. "Uh..."

Ben wondered if there was an answer anywhere on the planet soft enough to turn away the wrath of the giant bumble bee.

With a snort of disgust, Liz jerked out the purse hiding in the folds of fat under her arm, opened it, and pulled a pack of Camels out. She slapped the pack.

"Liz, please, I've asked you not to smoke in here."

Liz lifted her eyes as she pulled a cigarette out of the pack, and pinned Tru like a bug on a science fair display board.

"Liz, no smoking." Eleanor appeared at the top of the steps. She marched down the stairs with so much vigor, Ben hoped the risers had been fully reinforced. "Put that away unless you're planning to step outside. I don't even want it lit in here on your way out the door."

It occurred to Ben that Tru, a world-class wimp, surrounded

herself with strong-willed people. No soft answers coming out of *their* mouths. He wondered if he could work that tidbit of news into the twenty-page term paper she'd assigned him.

Liz's eyes narrowed as Eleanor reached the bottom step and crossed her arms.

Ben decided Liz was under control now, and he was more than ready to get out of this mad house. "Are you ready to go, Tru-Blue?"

"Don't call me that." Tru turned on him, the only person she sassed.

He tried to convince himself that made him special.

"Grab your shoes, and let's hit the road. I'm running late. You need a purse or anything?"

Tru looked around, spotted her briefcase and the books Ben had dropped off last night. She snatched the stack into her arms.

Ben relieved her of the load and decided to give the killer bee one tiny break just to help speed things up. "Look. I gave Tru a ride home last night, and I'm here to take her back."

Ben rested a hand gently but firmly on Tru's back and urged her out the door.

Ben heard Liz huffing along, following them. He glanced back and saw her pause to fire up her cigarette and take a long drag.

As she blew out a smoky cloud, she pointed the two fingers holding the cigarette at them. "Get back in here right this second."

Tru dug in her heels to stop. Ben hustled her along. The old bat was still yelling when Ben drove through the gate.

"Why did you do that? She's furious now." Tru looked at him, her eyes wide with fright.

"Who is that old bat?"

Tru gasped. "Don't talk about her that way."

"Why not?"

"Because she'll get mad." Tru looked behind her. They had left the driveway, but maybe Tru thought they were still too close. "And you wouldn't like her when she's mad."

Ben shrugged. "I don't like her now."

Tru flinched. "Next time you see her, be nice to her."

"No." Ben hit his blinker and pulled the truck into the fast lane.

"Please, Ben." Tru clutched her hands together as if she were prepared to beg. "Do it for me."

"Why?"

"Because I'm scared of her."

"Why?"

Tru was silent for a minute. "Because she's scary."

Ben had to give her that. "So, who is she and why did she have a key to your house?"

Tru gasped. "She used her key? I left the door unlocked for her. She gets upset when she has to use her key."

"I locked it when I came in. And, it looked like she came pre-upset so what difference does the lock make. Who is she?"

"She's my business manager."

Ben swerved. For a second, he thought he was going airborne off an overpass. He got the truck back in in its lane to the sound of blaring horns.

"You mean she works for you?" His voice was so loud, it hurt his eardrums.

"Of course. Why else would she have a key to my house?"

"I wondered if she was your mother."

Tru gasped so loud it was almost a scream. "*That woman is not my mother.*"

"At least if she were your mother, it would explain why you put up with her. Since she works for you, and you're terrified of her, here's a thought: why don't you fire her fat, striped..."

"I can't fire her."

"Is she blackmailing you?"

"No. I just can't fire her because it would be..."

Ben knew what she was going to say. "She's your case study for all your books. Man, that must be exhausting. You have to practice giving a soft answer to all that wrath, all the time?"

Tru nodded. "Besides, she needs the work, and she's good at her job."

"What does a business manager do?" Ben thought if the woman did only bookwork and accounting, maybe Trudy didn't cross paths with her too often and, if Liz was honest and hard-working and could add and subtract, then...

"She arranges appearances on radio and television shows for me. She's my go-between with my agent and editors. She answers fan mail and talks to the people who call my hotline asking for counseling."

Ben stepped hard on the brake. Forty miles an hour was as fast as he dared drive during this conversation.

"You let that woman talk to actual, real-live people?"

"Well, Ben," Tru answered, crossing her arms. "What other kind of people are there?"

He eased onto the Interstate and headed north without coming even close to crashing but then he was a highly trained professional.

"Tru, she has *got* to be sending out exactly the wrong signals to everyone who wants to work with you. They call, expecting kind, soft-spoken Tru 'Intervention' Jennings, and they get Liz 'Killer Bee' Borden."

"Stop speaking so disrespectfully about her. She's my friend."

Ben snorted. The sound reminded him of class last night.

"And," she added, "snorting is unbecoming of a police officer."

It must have reminded her of class, too.

"Great, you yell at me but Liz gets a pass." Ben pulled off the Interstate and headed toward the university.

Tru turned to him, her eyes as wide as a deer's caught in an eighteen-wheeler's headlights. "I did yell at you, didn't I? That was wrong of me. I'm sorry."

"If you cry, I swear I'll pull this truck over and tan your backside. *Then* you'll have a reason to cry."

"You will not."

"Probably not," Ben admitted.

The watery glaze left her eyes as they narrowed. "I thought we were working on turning the other cheek."

"You're working on it. I'm not." Ben pulled into the university parking lot and pulled to a stop. "You know, we've been talking about all the wrong things on this drive."

Tru reached for the door handle.

He was disgusted with himself for getting sidetracked by Attila the Bee. "I need to tell you about Watson."

Her hand froze. "What about him?"

"We should have arrested him last night. He's got priors. He's done jail time for two violent offenses, both against girlfriends."

"He beat them?" Tru's manicured fingertips released the handle.

Ben nodded. "In public. He got a felony conviction both times because other people testified. Both women were going to let it slide."

"He said he was married and she left him." Tru's voice trembled.

"He is married and she did leave him." Ben had an uncharacteristic moment of sympathy for kind-hearted Tru. He knew what he had to tell her next would be upsetting. He reached over and patted her arm. He felt like a bull moose trying to comfort an abandoned duckling. One wrong move and he'd crush her.

"His wife left the hospital last April with a broken arm, a broken rib that punctured her lung, her nose and cheekbone shattered, and two black eyes. She went directly from the hospital to a battered women's shelter."

"Did she file charges?"

"She started to, but realized Watson fell under the three-strike rule."

"His third felony," Tru said. "Which means life."

"She refused to put him away. Now, because of *her* spineless, misplaced act of kindness, Watson is running around loose, free to come after you."

"Because he wants his wife back," Tru muttered.

"The wife he beat to a pulp. And because of *your* spineless, misplaced act of kindness, he's free to hassle you some more, wait around for his wife to surface, or pick a new lady friend to beat up. Somebody needs to get this guy off the streets."

Tru turned to him. She was listening at last. She was going to do the right thing. He sighed with relief.

"This man sounds like a classic case of moral poverty. I am not going to be the next in a long line of people who take advantage of him."

"Moral what? Poverty? Take advantage? Of what, for Pete's sake?" Ben felt like a boiling pot with the lid clamped tight, and he was just about ready to blow.

"When a child isn't given the advantage of loving, capable parenting, when a child grows up in surroundings that are fatherless, jobless, and Godless, then he's set on a path for just the kind of behavior Watson is manifesting."

"Manifesting?" Ben was tempted to shake her, which was something Watson might do. But Watson would do it for no good reason. With the kind of garbage that was coming out of Tru's mouth right now, Ben thought he could get off on a self-defense plea.

"The solution to the violence we see in Ralph," she continued, "is not incarceration but intensive therapy, rock-solid moral support and, most of all, love."

"Ralph?"

"Ralph Watson is his name."

*Now she's on a first-name basis with a wife beater?* "I know his name."

"We disrespect him by calling him Watson."

"That's fair. I definitely disrespect him."

"For me to press charges..."

Ben watched Tru touched her fingertips with feather-light gentleness to her bleeding heart. "When the man is so desperate and, if he's telling the truth..."

"Which he isn't." Ben had no doubt he was lying.

"Which I believe he *is*, then approaching me last night was a cry for help."

"There was no one crying in that parking lot but you, Tru-blue. He grabbed you." Ben reached over and turned her chin so he could see her scraped cheek. "He hurt you."

"He wants to change, Ben." She pulled away.

"He left you terrified and bleeding." Ben's jaw tightened when he looked at her wounded face.

"He loves his wife." Tru shook her head as if she were talking to a mentally-challenged fourth grader. "He knows he's been wrong."

"He ripped out a chunk of your hair."

"No, that happened because..."

"Okay, okay. So Little Goody Tru Shoes isn't going to press charges. Got it. Watson falls into your 'No Jerk Left Behind' program. You know what? You're just as bad as all those women he's been beating."

"I am not as bad as them." There was dead silence in the truck for a few moments. Then Tru added, "And they're not bad."

"So, they should have just stayed in there and taken their lumps from poor, misunderstood, amorally-infested Ralph, until they loved him into changing or died, whichever came first?"

"Manifested, not infested. And Moral Poverty is the correct term. And no, of course they shouldn't stay and be beaten. A woman can't stay in an abusive situation. She has to get herself to a safe place and work on the relationship from a position of strength. But he's not going to beat me. He wants me to help him."

"But he did beat you. You have bruises all over your body." Ben blew out a long breath, shaking his head. "He wants your help, but you sent him to someone else."

"That's how I helped him. I sent him to Dr. Pavil. Ralph most likely has a drug or alcohol addiction. Chances are good he is unemployed and not even looking for work anymore. I imagine he is living in abject poverty and is, in all probability, illiterate."

"He's an author." Ben thought of the report he'd been faxed at home that almost made him choke on his Wheaties this morning. "He made five hundred thousand dollars last year on royalties from three books."

"And poverty just adds to the pressure his marriage is under and goads his temper. So you see..." Tru stopped talking and leaned toward Ben and erupted. "He made five hundred thousand dollars last year?"

"Yep, in royalties alone. And he has every year for the last eight. I understand there are advances too. Besides that, he's smart with investments. He has a fat stock portfolio of blue chippers. Big into Muni Bonds. He lives in a place nicer than yours, Tru-blue. That's what his wife ran from."

"What kind of books does he write?"

Ben leaned over until his nose almost touched hers. "Whatever the voices in his head tell him to write."

Tru jerked away from him and cracked her head on the door behind her.

Ben forgot he was angry. "You all right?"

Tru rubbed her head, and Ben reached over to help.

Her hair drizzled like golden silk under his finger. And she smelled just the same as last night. A smell that Ben would like to declare illegal anywhere near him because he was getting addicted as surely as if it was a street drug.

He moved away from her.

"I'm fine." She smoothed her neat blond ponytail.

Ben nodded. She was, indeed, very, very fine. "Go to work, Tru-Blue. When's your last class?"

"I'm finished at four-thirty today."

"No more night classes?"

"Just the Monday night class."

"And all your classes are in the Psycho Building?"

"Yes. And it's not the Psycho Building."

"I'll be here waiting at four-thirty."

"Okay." Tru opened the door, got out of the truck and turned back. "No, you won't."

"Don't argue with me, Tru. I'm your door-to-door escort service until I'm sure this nut is going to leave you alone."

"This nut is not going to bother me."

Ben could almost see her brain working as she thought that over. She finally added, "And he's not a nut."

"You're stuck with me. You kick up a fuss about it, and I'll tell the president of the university you've got a stalker, and I want you put on a leave-of-absence until the matter's resolved."

"Lloyd won't put me on leave on your say-so."

Ben arched one eyebrow. "I can be pretty persuasive."

She grunted. "Persuasive? You're obnoxious."

"Where's that soft answer when you're dealing with me, Tru-Blue? You let Watson pound on you. The giant killer bee pushes you around. Even Eleanor bullies you, although in a loving way. But me? You're mean to me."

She gave Ben that sad, on-coming-semi look again. "You're right, Ben. I'm so sorry. Of course, you can take me home. It's so nice of you to want to protect me. Please forgive me."

Ben laughed in her face. "Not persuasive, huh?"

Tru's teeth clenched.

"I got you to ride home with me last night, didn't I?"

"Yes, but that was because..."

"And I got you to ride back with me this morning, didn't I?"

"My car was here, what was I supposed to..."

"And I'm picking you up at four-thirty, aren't I?"

"Yes, but that doesn't mean..."

Ben reached across the seat and grabbed the handle of her door. "Good girl. I'll see you at then. Don't wander around the campus alone. Don't stay in an empty building. And don't keep me waiting." He slammed the door in her face.

"Ben Garrison," she yelled through the closed door. "I don't need a ride home and I wouldn't..."

Ben's window slid down. He said with the best false sincerity he could manage, "Are you mad at me, Tru?" He did his best to look worried and hurt.

Ben could actually see her melting. He tried to think of a way to toughen her up, except with him. He wanted her to be marshmallow soft for him.

"I'm sorry I'm so irritable this morning, Ben. I keep taking it out on you, and I apologize."

"See you at four-thirty, Tru-Blue." He grinned so she'd know he got her again.

Her jaw tightened, but she didn't say, "Don't bother."

He laughed all the way to the precinct.

He couldn't help liking Tru Jennings.

# CHAPTER SEVEN

TRUDY COULDN'T STAND BEN GARRISON.
She scowled all the way to her office.

"What happened to your face?" Her secretary Ethel stood from behind her desk, her eyes flicking back and forth between the scrape on Trudy's face and the frown on her lips. Trudy realized one was as unusual as the other.

Ethel whipped around her desk and adjusted her thick bifocals to get a good close look.

Trudy's first instinct was to tell her secretary to mind her own business. She battled for control of her temper, something she'd never had to do before she met Ben. Of course she'd met Ralph Watson about the same time, she felt like this was Ben's fault but it might be more complicated than that.

"I had a run-in last night with the brick wall outside this building. A man came up to me in the dark and frightened me, although he just wanted to talk." Trudy ran one hand down her upper arms. She'd worn a long-sleeved sweater today, despite the Texas August heat. Short sleeves would have shown the shocking bruises.

"Have you seen a doctor? I remember once, I'd just had my first baby, and I was walking the floor at night and, in the dark, I tripped over a rattle my no-account husband Jeeter had left on the floor."

"Jeeter would be your first husband?" Trudy's head throbbed on the side where the building had slapped her.

"Second. Stanley was first, but he was in and gone so fast," Ethel snapped her fingers as if to dismiss the man, which it appeared she had. "I rarely speak of him."

Trudy had only heard about Stanley a couple hundred times. He didn't even begin to rank with Jeeter, or Ronnie, or Artie. Trudy thought that was all the marriages Ethel had managed in her sixty years. "I'm running late, Ethel. I've got to..."

"I'll hurry then. I tripped on the rattle, almost dropped the baby, and, trying to save myself, I whacked my face on the wall. Well, I screamed for..."

Trudy started outlining the next chapter of *Tru Intervention: Bullies*. Her books were two hundred pages. At the rate she was writing, and if her insomnia hung on, she should be done with the first draft by the end of the week.

"Then Archie said..."

"I thought you were talking about Jeeter."

Ethel gave her a fussy look. She was a master of them. She plunked her hands on her non-existent hips. "Pay attention. This is the second accident. Archie was always late for dinner, so one time I took the frying pan and turned it..."

Trudy thought about Ben's overbearing behavior. He had no business ordering her to ride home with him. She had a good mind to be gone when he arrived. Except she couldn't leave before her last class, which ended at four o'clock.

Ethel's tight gray curls quivered with annoyance. "So, Ronnie just stood there and laughed. Can you believe that?"

Trudy thought they were still on Archie, but she knew better than to ask questions. "How rude."

"Well, that was Ronnie, all over. My knee still hurts when it's going to rain."

Trudy had heard that tragic news a number of times.

The office door whisked open. Gordan Wells stalked in wearing his full security guard regalia. Some of the security guards relaxed and dressed in blue jeans, but never Gordan. Of course, it was possible they didn't make blue jeans big enough for Gordan.

"I got special orders this morning to keep an eye on you, Trudy. The Long Pine PD called and...what happened to your face?"

So Trudy had to listen to Ethel's story about her many injuries again. She considered it direct intervention from God when the clock ticked toward time for her first class. "Well, I've got to run."

"Don't you want to hear about the time Jeeter..."

"You've never said what happened to your face." Gordan followed her out of the room.

Ethel was still talking as Trudy speed-walked down the hall, a few minutes early but excited to get somewhere that had students who were often very quiet. Many of them tried to sneak in a nap in the morning classes. She would appreciate their silence today.

"I'm waiting right outside this door, Trudy. I'm not budging an inch."

"No, Gordan." Trudy turned to the corpulent young man whose thick glasses would seem to disqualify him from any security detail. "You're not expected to do that."

"No, problem. Glad to do it."

Trudy took a step toward the classroom. Gordan's arm shot out, blocking her way as if a speeding train were bearing down on them. He whispered, "Let me go in first."

Trudy's eyes fell closed and she shook her head. She looked up to see Gordan, all three hundred pounds of him, tiptoeing into the empty room. He looked behind the door. Trudy was relieved they didn't issue weapons to campus security guards.

Gordan checked the room thoroughly for hidden criminals.

When he was satisfied, he stationed himself outside the door with his hands folded in front of him in die-hard, bodyguard fashion. "You can go in now. It's safe."

Trudy rolled her eyes. A movement down the hall drew her attention.

A man stood silhouetted against a glass door. Against the outside light, she couldn't make out any features but she felt the heat of his gaze. Terror grabbed her just as Watson's hands had last night.

It was Watson. He spun around and darted out the door.

Trudy turned to Gordan. He was still staring straight ahead and hadn't noticed a thing. She grabbed his arm. "Did you...?

Gordan jumped, screamed like a nine-year-old girl and whirled around. "What? What happened?" He clawed at his belt like he expected to find a holster. He managed to pull a Chapstick out of his pocket. Fully armed, he said, "What is it?"

Trudy looked from the Chapstick to Gordan's sweet, chubby face. She looked back at the hallway. Empty.

Now that the man was gone, she wasn't quite sure what she'd seen. She shuddered and stared at that door, willing herself to regain her composure and think. In the end, she had to admit she wasn't sure if it was Watson or a janitor. "I just don't know," she whispered.

"Don't know what?" Gordan noticed what he was holding and clenched his fist around the tube, as if hoping she hadn't noticed it wasn't a gun.

Even if it were Watson, he was just trying to contact her again. She sniffed in disgust. *The man could just phone my office for an appointment like a normal human being.*

"Don't know what?" Gordan repeated.

Trudy breathed in and out until she controlled her fear. The first student appeared through the glass entry door where Watson—or the janitor, as the case may be—had disappeared.

"My class."

"You don't know about your class?" Gordan put on some Chapstick.

"That's what I said, Gordan. But now that I think about it, of course I know about my class. I'm teaching from a book I wrote, for heaven's sake." She smiled and went into her room.

Trudy got through the day, thankful for students and good-hearted but weak-minded bodyguards. At three fifty-five, she dismissed her last 'Abnormal Psych 402' session of the day and headed for the sanctuary of her office.

Ethel was gathering up her purse. "I've got to leave early, Trudy."

Which was fine with Trudy. Ethel was mostly for decoration anyway. Trudy did all her own paperwork and answered her own phone most of the time. Ethel always had something that took precedence over her secretarial work, like lunch, or family emergencies, or her fingernails.

"I've filled out the forms for my quarterly employee evaluation. I signed them for you and sent them to the dean's office."

Trudy couldn't believe what she'd just heard. "Did you say you forged my signature?"

"Well, of course I did. All secretaries do it."

*No, they don't. And the only reason you did it is to give yourself a good evaluation.*

*Soft answer. Soft answer.* With a weak smile pasted on her face, Trudy said, "Ethel, it's against the rules for anyone but me to fill out that form."

Ethel waved her hand as if the rules were a pesky fly buzzing around her head. "I'm just saving you from doing the chore."

*It's the first chore you ever saved me from, you old...*

Trudy breathed in and out. She wasn't usually this short tempered. Somehow it seemed right to blame Ben, although getting attacked might be the cause.

While she fished for a soft answer, Ethel went on as chipper as a song bird. "I put myself in for a raise. I've been with the university for two years now and I'm due. I've been with five professors in my years here, so I'm really experienced. I deserve some recognition for all my hard work."

"Five professors in two years?" Trudy remembered when Ethel had been assigned to her. The dean had failed to meet her eyes squarely. Now she knew why.

Trudy took a second to figure out whose aunt Ethel was. "Have you always gotten good evaluations?"

"What kind of question is that?" Ethel bristled.

*What I want to know is have you forged all your evaluations and is that the only reason you're still here?*

"I didn't mean anything by it. I'm just asking." Trudy wished she could retract the question because she knew Ethel wouldn't let it drop.

"I work hard for you every day. I come in here, maybe not always before you, but eventually. Not everybody has such a faithful secretary. Why, I know people who have jobs and just plain don't show up. How'd you like to have someone like that working here?"

*And exactly how would that be different?*

Trudy wasn't sure why she was having a sudden attack of sarcasm of the brain. She was only sure it was wrong and she was failing. *God, I'm sorry. Help me come up with a soft answer here.* The best she could manage was, "I wouldn't like that at all."

Ethel's blue-tinged gray hair quivered with anger. "That's right, you wouldn't, and don't you forget it. I can't believe how ungrateful you're being." She slapped her purse under her arm and whirled to leave.

"Wait," Trudy said.

Ethel whirled back around. The song bird had turned into a little gray-haired bull, and Trudy wanted to wave a red cape.

"Don't go away angry, please." She braced herself for whatever

Ethel had to say. She'd turn the other cheek. She'd take whatever slings and arrows Ethel sent flying her way.

*Don't go away angry, just go away.*

Trudy shook her head to clear it of this strange new sarcastic attitude. "The evaluation is fine this time, and so is the signature. I didn't think of discussing it with you, and I apologize for that. If all the other secretaries do it, I can imagine how you'd think I wouldn't mind."

Trudy kept her voice calm but she couldn't quite roll over so far as to give Ethel permission to commit forgery. "I do mind, though. From now on, in this office, I'll sign things myself."

"Well, all you had to do was say so," Ethel said with a huff. "If you want to put up with all the tedious forms in this office, it's nothing to me."

*I'm already doing them myself. This is the first time you've ever...*

"If that's all you had to say, I'll be going now." Ethel walked away as if she were a queen who had granted a commoner an audience.

Trudy watched her leave, wondering how many ways her secretary was going to find to punish her for this over the next few months.

When the door clicked shut, it echoed in the empty hallways.

Most classes ended at four. Trudy wondered if there were any people left in the building. She hurried to the door Ethel had exited through and looked outside. Even her faithful bodyguard Gordan was gone.

Trudy glanced quickly at her watch. Four-fifteen. Ben would be here in fifteen minutes.

If she hadn't promised to wait for him, she'd run out of the building and race for home.

Instead, she went into her own office and pulled some notes together for the next day. That finished, she phoned a local grocery store to order supplies for tonight, glanced at her watch, and decided she had time before Ben arrived to clean out her email.

*"Give me what I want."*

The subject line popped up on the screen. The words hit her like a fist. She didn't have to open it to know what it would say.

*"Give me what I want, or I'll take it."*

A second message appeared.

*"Give me what I want."*

Messages kept appearing. Seconds ticked by as the number rose to five, then ten, then twenty—all of them with the same subject line.

*"Give me what I want."*

She began opening them by rote, hoping one of them would say something else. Fearing one of them would say something else. Her stomach twisted as each message appeared.

*"Give me what I want, or I'll take it."*

Watson's words. It was him. It had to be. There was no other message. If he'd have asked her a question, or given her a contact number, she'd have done her best to help the man.

*"Give me what I want."*

Each time a new e-mail popped into view, her nerves wound tighter.

*"Give me what I want."*

Her breath caught in her throat and her heart pounded harder as the number climbed to 25, 26, 27.

*"Give me what I want."*

She should contact him.

*"Give me what I want."*

She should scream for help.

*"Give me what I want."*

She should try and help the poor man.

*"Give me what I want."*

She should hire a full-time bodyguard, a meaner one than Gordan.

*"Give me what I want."*

There was a sharp rap on her office door.

She shrieked and whacked her knees on the bottom of her desk when she jumped and cried out in pain.

The door slammed open and Ben rushed in, his gun drawn. He wheeled around the room, gun extended.

"What happened?" He kept the gun drawn but raised it to the ceiling, beside one ear. His eyes narrowed when he looked at her and crossed her small office in a couple of fast steps.

"What was it? What made you scream?"

Trudy realized she had goosebumps everywhere.

"Did he show up here today? Did he hurt you again?" Ben rubbed her arm.

He'd noticed her crawling skin. He seemed to notice everything. She appreciated the comforting touch.

His gentleness pulled her out of the sick fascination she'd felt for the blitz of e-mails.

She raised her hands to cover her cheeks, wondering what he'd seen on her face to send him across the room so quickly.

"No, he didn't hurt me." She wondered why she had this knee jerk desire to protect poor, mixed up Ralph Watson. "It's just these e-mails. I'm on edge and when you knocked I was startled."

Startled...the understatement of the century so far.

Ben reached past her, crowding her sideways a little. He read the screen, scrolling through the remaining letters. "How many of these did you get?"

Trudy shrugged. "This isn't the first batch."

Ben rested a hand on her back. "They're from Watson, aren't they?"

"They're not signed."

"What's the e-mail address?"

"They're all different." She knew she should move aside. Get up and let Ben have the computer. But for right now, she needed the support of his warmth and strength.

Ben shook his head. "Anyone can get dozens of e-mail addresses. They're all those freebie kind. Look at these *takeit339@baddyemail. com*, *takeit340@baddyemail.com*. They're all like that. It's the same guy."

"I know that."

Ben looked away from the screen to stare down at her. His eyes were fierce, but they softened as she looked at him.

"I'm sorry, Tru-Blue. I'm sorry this sick-o scared you."

Trudy nodded. "Me, too."

Ben lifted his hand and brushed wisps of hair off her forehead. "You know it's Watson.

Trudy nodded, shrugged, nodded again. "Just one more thing we can't prove, right?"

"We could prove it with a search warrant."

"Could you get a search warrant with what happened last night?"

Ben's jaw tightened. His mouth formed a straight line. "Maybe."

"And what if it's just some other whack-o fan? Somebody who thinks it's funny to send harassing e-mails to the poor, stupid, pacifist author."

"Then we'll get him, too."

"And I'll have destroyed any chance I had of helping Ralph Watson."

Ben was silent for a long minute. "You know it's him. He hasn't tried to approach you today, has he?"

Tru hesitated a second too long.

Ben's eyes zeroed in on Trudy until she felt like they were boring into her skull. "He came here? Did he threaten you? Did he put his hands on you?"

"No, no he didn't come here. At least...well, once I thought I saw him at a distance, but it could have been somebody else."

"Were you alone?"

"I haven't been alone all day. My own private security guard was with me."

Ben nodded, his eyes squinting. "I noticed there wasn't anyone in your outer office just now. Did Watson contact your colleague?"

Ethel chose that moment to poke her head in the door and say with an irritable temper, "I forgot my sweater. You distracted me when I was leaving." She ducked back out.

"Get back here." Ben grabbed the door and opened it.

Ethel arched her eyebrows. "What's the problem?"

"Weren't you told that Dr. Jennings wasn't to be left alone?" Ben stood with his back to Trudy, but she could see the annoyance in the set of his shoulders. "I asked security to make that clear to the people who work with her."

"Sure, I heard that, but I'm always done for the day at four. I can't wait around."

"You've got a child to pick up at day care?" Ben asked.

Trudy rolled her eyes behind his back. No way did he think blue-haired, sixty-something Ethel had a child in day care.

"No," Ethel sniffed. She bent sideways to look past Ben's shoulder and glare at Trudy. Ethel held a grudge for weeks when she got annoyed. "I don't have any children in day care."

"You have a husband stranded somewhere, waiting for you to pick him up from work?"

"No, I just like to beat rush hour traffic. If I wait around after four, I might as well crawl home."

"So, Dr. Jennings' safety and a request from campus security mean less to you than avoiding a traffic jam?"

"Trudy, tell this wise-guy that I always go home at four."

Trudy heard the threat. She winced when she thought of the cold shoulder she'd have to endure if she thwarted Ethel twice in one day. Besides it was true. "She always goes home at four."

Ben was silent. He faced away from Trudy. Ethel looked away from Trudy with a satisfied smirk.

Whatever Ethel saw in Ben's expression, the smirk faded.

Ben crossed his arms. "You also weren't at your desk when I arrived. So, you came in here, saw her with a strange man, and said good-bye without giving it a second thought."

With a sullen shrug, Ethel said, "I'll wait until Trudy leaves the building."

"As it happens, now that I'm here, it will be fine if you leave."

"Then why'd you make such a big deal about it?"

"I didn't," Ben said.

Trudy noticed his tense neck muscles didn't match the mild tone of his voice. She wondered what would happen if Ben decided to make a big deal out of something.

"I just asked if you were aware of the security request so I'd know if you hadn't been informed or if you were deliberately ignoring the order."

"Okay, tomorrow I stay until you show up or she leaves. Satisfied?" Ethel swung the door shut with a sharp snap.

Ben reached for it.

"Let her go." Trudy jumped up and rounded her desk. "Please, Ben."

Ben turned to her and shook his head in disgust. "So, yet another person who bullies you. Do you see a trend here, Tru-Blue?"

Trudy wrinkled her nose at him.

"Let's get out of here. We're going to the police station to swear out a complaint against Watson. Then, I'm going to make sure you get home safe. Once you're locked down for the night, I'll have a squad car..."

"I've got church tonight." Trudy glanced at her watch. "Yikes, I'm supposed to be there by five. I've got to get going."

Grabbing her briefcase and purse, she dodged Ben and reached for the door.

He caught her arm. "You're not going to church. You're going to the precinct. We're going to get a line on this guy once and for all."

"I'm the chairman of the Casserole Committee. I've got to go and make twenty pans of lasagna tonight. The committee depends on me. I've already ordered the groceries and I need to pick them up. If I don't move right now, I'll be late."

Ben let her go and plunked his fists on his hips. "Call someone and tell them you can't make it."

"Better yet," Tru snipped. "Get yourself into gear, and come with me. I could use the help. We're always short-handed. We'll deal with the police later."

Tru stormed out of her office.

Ben growled at her heels like a junkyard dog. "The longer you wait to press charges, the weaker your case becomes. It's already been close to twenty-four hours. The bruises on your face will go a long way toward convincing a judge to issue a warrant for his arrest."

Tru marched out of the building and came to an abrupt stop. "My car's been stolen."

"No, it hasn't. I had a uniformed officer drive it to your home earlier today." Ben drew even with her.

Tru whirled and crossed her arms. "How did you get my keys?"

"I didn't have to get them. You left them in the ignition. Stop doing that, by the way. Haven't you ever heard the saying, 'Don't help a good boy go bad?'"

Ben pointed at his truck parked nearby.

She glared at the truck, then at Ben.

"You said you'd let me give you a ride home, Tru-Blue."

When he used that wheedling voice on her, she just melted. She had to get a backbone. "I've got to go to church. We use those casseroles to feed people just home from the hospital and families who have a new baby. We also deliver them when there's a death in the family. If I don't do this, the need is going to be felt right away."

She rested her hand on his arm. "Please, Ben? This is important. It's got to take priority over having Ralph arrested. And you're here with me, so I'm safe." Trudy was amazed to hear wheedling coming from her own lips. She didn't think of herself as a wheedling kind of gal.

Ben sighed and dropped his head until his chin rested on his chest. "We need to get this guy, Tru. You're not safe while he's on the street."

Trudy tightened her grip on his arm. "Is my safety more important than a hungry family? Is it more important than letting grieving
people know their church family loves them?"

"Yes."

"No."

Ben shook his head as if he were exhausted. "Okay, Tru-Blue.
Turn off the violins. I'll go with you, and I'll stay and help cook
up a bunch of casseroles with your church group. When's your first
class in the morning?"

"I don't have to be in until eleven."

"Can we please file a complaint against this guy first thing in
the morning?"

Tru thought of Liz and Ethel bullying her. Ben was as strong-
willed as Liz and Ethel combined, yet he was going to let her
decide this issue. It was a heady experience. It also occurred to her
than she didn't demand anything from Liz and Ethel. She wondered what would happen if she laid down the law.

"Thanks." She smiled up at her personal bodyguard. "Thanks for
letting the decision be mine. I think I should file charges against
him. It might protect the next woman he decides to hurt."

"No, Tru, thank you for agreeing to go in." Ben took her arm
and led her to his truck. "Let's go get those groceries."

# CHAPTER EIGHT

"WHERE'S THE COMMITTEE?" BEN STAGGERED under the weight of the groceries. He looked around the empty parking lot. "I was hoping a dozen ladies would all come rushing out to meet us and help us haul this stuff in."

Tru came along beside him, carrying three grocery bags. "Five of us are on the committee. They must be late."

"Five would help," Ben said.

Tru hefted the case of spaghetti sauce jars and Ben relieved her of them. They weighed a ton. He took plastic grocery bags in each hand, too. "We'll be lucky to make it in another two trips if we load ourselves down this much every time."

"Ben, don't whine. It isn't attractive." Trudy pulled the heavy church door open with one finger. One of his bags was slipping, but he just held on tighter and didn't complain. Not after that whining crack. "Lead the way for your humble pack mule, Dr. Tru." He clung to the bags.

They made it to the kitchen. "I'll get the rest of it. You start cooking." Ben headed for the door.

"No, I insist on helping. You'll be in and out several times if you have to do it alone."

"I'm fine, Tru. Just get busy."

Tru caught the sleeve of his white button-down shirt.

He was a big strong man. He turned to her, to reassure her of that. Furrows across her brow stopped him. "What's the matter?"

Tru shrugged and dropped her hand. Speaking to the floor, she said, "It's just that...when we got here, the church wasn't locked and I don't know if I want to...to stay in here." She looked up at him. "All alone."

Ben's heart melted. "Come on. I didn't want to do it by myself anyway. I just didn't want to whine anymore."

A bright smile lit up her face. "Trying to cut back on the whining is admirable."

"Get moving, smart Alec." Ben waved her out of the kitchen.

Loaded down once more, Ben asked, "How were you going to get all these groceries in the Seville?"

Tru shrugged. "I would have managed."

They got the last load in, and Ben locked the church door. "Is the rest of this place wide open?"

Tru nodded. "If you lock it, the rest of the Casserole Committee won't be able to get in."

Ben looked back at the lock. "It'd take me all night to search the place and make sure Watson isn't already inside. We'd never get the lasagna done."

Looking around the vast building, he added, "But as for worrying about the rest of the committee, they're already a half hour late. No one is coming but us." Facing the futility of it, Ben left the door unlocked.

Tru led the way to the kitchen.

"How many people belong to this church?"

"Two thousand."

"And not one of them could show up to help you with the casseroles?"

She tugged a huge stack of aluminum pans out of a bag and ripped open the first of two ten-pound packages of hamburger. "Would you lay four lasagna noodles in the bottom of each pan while I get the hamburger started browning?"

Ben learned more than he wanted to know about lasagna. He also saw Tru jump every time a board creaked in the big, empty church. Ben didn't like the sound of some of those creaks either. No building settled that much.

Two hours later, he set the last pan of lasagna in the church's freezer with a sigh of relief. "I'm exhausted. Jesus might have been able to feed five thousand people with no trouble, but it's not so easy for me."

Tru smiled at him. Red sauce splattered on her apron made her look like Little Suzy Homemaker, not a tenured professor and wealthy author.

"It's done for another month, anyway." She took off her apron and balled it up. Ben looked down at his dishpan hands as Tru put the last frying pan away, scrubbed and wiped dry. Then she gathered up every towel, washcloth and apron in the kitchen and stuffed them in one of her empty grocery bags.

"What are those for?" Ben asked.

"I'll wash them up and bring them back." She led the way out of the church.

"You have to do the church's laundry, too?"

She looked over her shoulder as she reached for the outside door. "When I get something dirty, I clean it up."

Ben reached past her and held the door closed. "Let me go out first."

Tru jumped back and gave the door a frightened look.

He knew, despite her hard work and cheerful attitude, that she'd been on edge all evening. He swung the door open. Staring out at the night, he stood until his eyes adjusted to the darkness. He stepped out, keeping Tru close behind him.

"Ben, is this necessary?"

"Are we locking this door?" He still held onto her, which he hoped more than answered the question of whether he thought this was necessary.

"No."

"Bleeding hearts," Ben snorted. "You make it easy for a kid to get in trouble."

He towed Tru along in his wake, keeping a close eye on a clump of bushes in the corner of the parking lot. They swayed a bit more than could be explained away by the night breeze. He lifted Tru by the waist and settled her in the front seat. She didn't even suggest climbing into the truck herself this time.

When Ben got behind the wheel, she said, "You know, that crack about bleeding hearts almost sounds like my third book, in which I deal extensively with moral poverty."

"I read *Tru Interventions: Criminals.*"

"Have you read all my books?"

"It's a bunch of hooey." He rolled down his window as he sat in the truck.

Tru sputtered, and he couldn't stop a grin from breaking out. It gave him away.

"You're tormenting me for entertainment, aren't you?"

Impatient with wondering why the bushes rustled, Ben pulled his cell phone out.

"Who are you calling?"

The dispatcher came on the phone before he could answer Tru's question. He identified himself. "I'm at East Pelham Street, in the south lot of the Christ United Church. I'm ready to leave, but there may be suspicious activity in the bushes here. The woman I'm with is being stalked, and I want someone to check this out. I don't want to leave her alone while I do it."

Tru yanked on his arm. "You don't know I'm being stalked."

"Roger, that," the dispatcher responded.

He switched the phone to his other ear so she could yank to her heart's content and not interrupt his call.

The dispatcher sent a cruiser in his direction.

"You're being stalked. Two physical encounters, the e-mails. What would you call it?"

"We don't know those e-mails came from Ralph."

Ben shrugged. "Maybe you're being stalked by two people. Lucky girl. I'm betting it's all Watson. And if he's lurking in those bushes over there, I want him caught."

Tru's eyes stormed.

"What are you thinking, Tru-Blue? That you ought to run over and warn him?"

Tru looked at the bushes. "You really think there's someone in there?"

Tru jumped at a sudden, frantic movement in the hedge and grabbed Ben's forearm.

"He's taking off. I've got to stop him." Ben reached for the door handle.

Tru threw herself toward him across the console and coiled her arms around his neck. "Don't go out there. He might hurt you."

The contact redirected his attention. Holding this trembling, sweet-smelling woman would be enough to distract a magnet from true north. He hadn't held a woman close since Cara. And he'd fully intended never to do it again. Trudy reminded him of Cara in the worst possible way. She was soft. Soft and sweet, without a mean bone in her body.

He didn't blame Cara for cutting her losses. She wasn't the first woman who couldn't handle a cop's life.

Most of his friends were married to tough, self-sufficient women. Ben had admitted long ago that he was most attracted to softies, like Cara and Tru. That was just his nature. And he'd learned to ignore his interest in that type of woman because they couldn't handle his job.

That left him with no one, which suited him fine. And Tru, holding him, protecting him from whatever that bush hid, was twice as soft as Cara inside and out. He eased her away from him as the noise in the bushes faded and running footsteps pounded on the sidewalk, fading away by the time Ben got his door open.

"He's gone." Disgusted for letting Tru divert him, he tightened his jaw. "I missed another chance to catch the jerk."

A cruiser pulled into the lot.

Ben got out, folded up the center arm rest and dragged Tru across the seat behind him to get down on his side. He didn't want her out of arm's reach, even for a moment.

He talked to the uniformed cop for a while and the three of them, because he wasn't letting Tru leave his side, looked through the bushes.

"A lot of footprints, Detective." The uniform pointed his heavy flashlight at the ground.

Ben crouched and ran a finger over the tell-tale marks. "This isn't close enough to any path for these footprints to be left here by a pedestrian. Someone was standing in these bushes."

"Yeah, and it rained in the night last night," the young policeman said. "These tracks are fresh."

Ben stood and turned to Tru. "It's him. It's Watson. You know it is."

Tru seemed to shrink as she stood in the dim glow of the flashlight.

"He was probably inside the church tonight. All that creaking we heard wasn't the sound of the Holy Ghost. If you'd gone there alone to cook, who knows what would have happened."

"What do we do now, Ben?"

Even for his soft-hearted Tru, she sounded too obedient. This wasn't fair. Tru only wanted to love everybody. He should have moved faster. He should have nabbed Watson.

"We file charges. I know you have doubts about exactly what he's guilty of, but when he put his hands on you, he committed assault. Even if he weasels out of the charges this time, we'll be able to arrest him if he tries to approach you again." Ben felt Tru's shudder.

"Approach me? You mean attack me." Tru turned her blue eyes on him.

Ben wanted to slay dragons for her. But he could be her defender without getting stupid and wanting more.

*God, please protect her.* "He doesn't have to attack you for it to qualify as harassment. Once you file, we can get a search warrant and trace all those e-mail addresses to his home computer. We can use the proof of harassment to make the assault charge stick. First degree assault is a felony. We may be able to invoke the three strikes rule. For once, we might not have to wait until *after* some crack-pot commits a crime to protect a victim."

Tru nodded. "If I don't do something, he'll just go on hurting women. I'll press charges."

Ben sighed with relief. He took Tru's arm. "Let's get you home."

# CHAPTER NINE

"YOU DON'T NEED TO WALK me in, Ben." Trudy held her breath while he pulled to a stop.

As usual, he ignored her wishes. "No bother."

Her knees wobbled with relief. Her stupid pink house glowed in the artificial light. She wondered how she'd ended up with this monstrosity. An investment, that's how Liz had persuaded her. An investment just like the Seville.

"Wait until I get your door for you." Ben came around and let her out.

He shielded her from the shrubbery that lined her fenced-in yard. His eyes were cool and observant as he escorted her to the house.

It made Trudy sick to realize he was shielding her from danger with his own body.

"I'm going to make sure there's no one inside before I leave, so don't bother complaining about it." Ben took Trudy's key but the door swung open and Eleanor met them, armed with a cast iron skillet.

Trudy realized for the first time that Eleanor could be in danger, too. "You shouldn't be here alone."

Eleanor sniffed. She exchanged a glance with Ben.

"She's right." Ben nodded at the skillet. "Although I'd give you good odds in a fight. Who else can you get in here during the day?"

Eleanor whacked the back of the skillet against the flat of her hand. "Even alone, I'm quite a few people."

Ben grinned, then laughed out loud.

Eleanor jerked the skillet toward a huge bouquet of red roses on the table near the base of the sweeping staircase. "Before you go, that came today. I don't suppose you sent them."

Ben's easy-going smile shrank like a cheap T-shirt in a hot dryer. "Was there a card?"

"Nothing." Eleanor approached the flowers. "And we got five more letters in the mail today. Normally, I just sort the mail and give most of it to Liz but today, considering what happened last night, I opened them myself. I was careful about fingerprints."

"Glad you're on my side, Eleanor." Ben pulled a handkerchief out of his back pocket and picked up the closest letter. Trudy looked over his shoulder and read the dreaded words.

*'Give me what I want, or I'll take it.'*

Those were the only words on the letters spread out on the table around the roses.

Trudy rubbed her chest with an open palm.

When Ben glanced at her, she saw his eyes sharpen as he rested his hand on her shoulder.

"What company delivered them?" Ben looked back at the flowers.

"I made the delivery driver give me a card."

Eleanor produced it from the ample patch pocket of her blue floral top. While Ben studied it, Trudy tried to see the roses for their beauty and not as a threat.

He slipped the card into his shirt pocket and produced two of his own. He scribbled on both of them. "Good work. Next time call me right away." He gave one card to Eleanor, and handed a second one to Trudy. "The number I wrote down will always reach me. I can't always answer right away but I'll call back within minutes."

Eleanor frowned. "I should have phoned you when they arrived. The florist might have remembered something if you'd talked to him right away."

"You did okay. Trudy agreed to press charges against Watson. I'm taking her into the station tomorrow to file a formal complaint." Ben told Eleanor about the incident at church.

"I can tell you're taking this seriously, Eleanor. I doubt if you'd miss anything, but I'm still checking the house out before I leave."

"You won't hear *me* trying to stop you." Eleanor nodded.

*'Like Trudy keeps doing.'* Eleanor didn't say it out loud, but Trudy

got the message. Clenching her jaw, she watched the two of them take charge of her.

"Are you staying here tonight again?" Ben produced a zip lock bag from the inside pocket of his suit. He eased the letters inside and slipped the bag into his coat pocket.

Eleanor nodded. "I'm planning on sleeping here until this mess is cleared up."

"Good." He started toward the back of the house. "Thanks."

Trudy wondered why Ben never approved of anything *she* did.

A few minutes later, he walked down the stairs, snagged the roses, and headed for front door.

Turning, he looked at Trudy as if she were a recalcitrant child. "I'll be here at nine in the morning to take you to the station. Don't make me wait."

The same words as last night. He turned to leave, then paused. "What time does Liz get here?"

"Eight." Trudy remembered Liz was mad. The woman knew how to hold a grudge. "Maybe we should go in earlier. I don't want to be late for class."

"Eight. Good. I want to talk to her. I want to know why she hasn't said anything about these letters, assuming there have been more." He looked directly at Trudy. "I don't like her attitude."

"Few do," Eleanor agreed.

Trudy gasped.

Ben left as she opened her mouth to forbid him to upset her business manager further.

Eleanor huffed, "High time someone had a talk with that woman."

"We don't need to talk to her," Trudy said.

"Sure we do."

Trudy scowled. "If you think we need to talk to her, why haven't you mentioned it before now?"

"I'm scared of her." Eleanor shrugged. "What's your excuse?"

Trudy's shoulders slumped. "Same."

"Maybe Ben can take her." Eleanor left the room.

"Guess who'll be standing in the crossfire when he tries." Trudy trudged upstairs, expecting another sleepless night.

Tru held up her glow-in-the-dark watch and waited for the second hand to reach zero. Then she started.

Alabama

Alaska

Arizona

Arkansas

California

Colorado

Connecticut

Her computer, the beast, sat silently, accusing her of being a quitter.

"I'm not. I just need sleep."

Delaware

Florida

Georgia

Hawaii

She could reel off all fifty states in under a minute. She could say the capitals without the states in 90 seconds and with the states in two minutes and twenty-eight seconds flat. She could do all the presidents in under three minutes. She'd timed herself. Often.

Texas

Indiana

Iowa

Kansas

Kentucky

The exercise was supposed to put her to sleep because it was so boring. She usually stayed awake, bored half to death but wide awake.

Louisiana

Maine

Maryland

Massachusetts

The beast was on stand-by. She resented the fact that her laptop could sleep, and she couldn't. At least it didn't taunt her with the scrolling message she used for her screen saver: *A soft answer turns away wrath, but a harsh word stirs up anger. Proverbs 15:1*

Instead, it just sat like a dejected pet, vibing messages to her: *'How dare you try and sleep? I'm ready to play. Come and pay attention to me.'*

"Great, now I'm making up dialogue between myself and my computer." Trudy twisted under the covers until they had her knotted up tight.

Michigan

Minnesota

Mississippi

Missouri

She was wide awake. Why fight the inevitable?

Slipping out of bed, she touched the pad on her computer and the machine seemed to smile triumphantly at her. "And Ben thinks Watson's crazy," she muttered. "How's that any different than me?"

She launched her e-mails.

Messages began popping up.

'Give me what I want, or I'll take it.'

Ten, fifteen, twenty – the emails kept coming.

Ben had told her to leave the one's she'd received earlier so he could track the sender. Added to them, her inbox grew and grew until she had nearly fifty emails with that same, ominous subject line.

In the dark room, she felt the shadows reaching out to grab her. Her throat closed as her computer screen filled.

'Give me what I want.'

It was him. Ralph Watson. Ben was right. The man was dangerous. After the emails finished loading, she left them for Ben without opening a single one. She closed her mail box and opened her book.

She spent time in prayer before beginning her writing but, even after her communion with God, she had trouble being compassionate to the bullies she was trying to save.

Somehow, as she worked, she began picturing bullies in a form she'd never thought of before. Instead of junior high age boys, Liz muscled her way into Trudy's head. Trudy tried to be kind to her, but her fingers typed out a book that wasn't so nice.

She wrote about adult bullies instead of children. Ethel came next. Then she faced off against Ben Garrison. She told him off for about two chapters before she got herself under control and did some serious deleting.

She hated to admit it, but it felt good to tell these bullies off, even if it was in secret, on her computer.

But the bully who most concerned her was Ralph Watson. He was too frightening to write about. *"You're being irrational. He didn't do anything to you. He was just upset."*

She knew he was dangerous. But she also knew he needed help. Seeking God in prayer, she forced herself to use the bedrock honesty that had made her books bestsellers. She typed, choosing each word with love.

When she at last saved her work, she'd written three thousand words and saved one thousand. Rubbing her burning eyes, she sat at the desk and wished this night away.

The bed mocked her.

"God, where is your peace?"

The alarm clock glared a red digital 3:09 at her. Four hours of sleep max, if she went to sleep right now.

Trudy got up from the computer, so tired, she weaved her way to the bed. At least her nighttime torture could be in a soft place.

She climbed into bed and mentally told Liz and Ethel off for another hour. After that she chased Ben around with a big stick. *Turn the other cheek, but carry a big stick.* Teddy Roosevelt meets Jesus Christ.

Every time she realized what she was doing, she prayed, and, before she knew it, she'd be after Ben with a stick again.

Trudy would have cried her heart out, thinking about how tired she'd be tomorrow, but she'd gotten over letting her insomnia make her quite that crazy.

Staring at the bedroom ceiling, she whispered, "I've been tired before. I'll be tired again. Big deal."

As a motto, it left a lot to be desired.

But it kept her from letting these sleepless nights get the best of her. The fault for her lack of sleep didn't lie with Ben or Liz or Ethel. She'd always had trouble sleeping, even as a child. So, she tried her soothing tricks again.

Washington

Adams

Jefferson

Madison

Monroe

Maybe she just needed someone to shake some sense into her.

# CHAPTER TEN

"SOMEBODY NEEDS TO SHAKE SOME sense into that woman," Ben muttered as he tried the door to Trudy's house the next morning. It was unlocked. That lit the fuse on his temper.

He glanced at his watch. He was early. Good, he'd be on hand when Liz came in.

He swung the door open, and Tru just about ran him down. Today's business-like, yet classy and beautiful outfit was navy blue slacks and blouse, the blazer was a blue tweed-y thing. Her hair the same polished pony tail. Ben was sensing a theme.

"We go right now, or I go in alone."

Ben reached for her but she slipped past him and headed for his truck. "Tru, I want to talk to Liz before we go."

She opened his truck door and looked over her shoulder. "We go now, Ben, or I get the Seville. I'm not waiting while you harass my employees."

She narrowed her eyes at him and looked so darn cute trying to boss him around, he decided to encourage her by obeying. She needed to have a little success being bossy. It might be better to talk to Liz later, maybe drop by for a little chat without Tru refereeing.

By the time they reached the police station, he was exhausted from listening to her cheerful view of the world.

Trudy was touched by Ben's interest in her theories, so she continued to explain them. "And so you see, it's the intense personal counseling for an extended period of time that proves to these people that someone cares. And that's what makes all the difference."

Trudy smiled at him, amazed that he was beginning to see things her way. God bless him, he was really sweet under his gruff exterior.

He rounded the truck and opened her door with all the chivalry of a knight in shining armor.

He took her arm. "Stay close to me, Tru-Blu. There can be some shady characters hanging around a police station."

"How thoughtful, Ben." He really was a gentleman, until he towed her behind him with all the finesse of a tug boat dragging a floundering ship into port.

The police station was raucous as Ben more or less goose-stepped her through the room, winding around crowded desks and stepping over scruffy feet in narrow aisles.

"Garrison," a man roared like a wounded buffalo out of an office. "I need that report yesterday."

"Yeah, yeah, you'll get it when you get it," Ben snarled as he dragged Trudy along without stopping.

The roaring man slammed his door so hard, the white glass window rattled.

Ben didn't look left or right as he towed her like she was under arrest. She'd have fought him except she was afraid to be separated from him in this room full of grumpy, handcuffed men and even grumpier police officers interrogating their prisoners.

Trudy was actually breathing hard from the quick pace. "Ben, don't you think we should..."

"Garrison, we've got two weeks' worth of paperwork backed up. We're going to lose our court date and have to..."

Ben's shouted reply didn't appear in any books on chivalry. Trudy knew, because she'd cut her teeth on King Arthur and the Knights of the Round Table.

Another bellowing man was left in the dust as Ben pulled her into an office with the name Lt. Scott Sheridan in chipped paint on the opaque white glass.

"She's filing a report, Loo." Ben kicked the door shut. "I've got her. We've got priors. I want a judge to issue a search warrant for..."

A black man who looked about Ben's age, dark hair cut so short it was almost shaved, slapped his hand over the receiver. "Can't you see I'm on the phone?"

"I told you about her. Tru Jennings. She was attacked."

"Get out of here, Ben. I've got to take this call. Wait outside for a second."

Ben reached across the desk of the man Trudy assumed was his direct superior and plucked the phone out of the Lieutenant's hand. Ben put the phone to his ear. "Call back in a half hour."

He hung up the phone with a sharp click. "We've got to move on this, Scott."

Scott Sheridan erupted from his desk. His chair skidded behind him and crashed into the wall. "That was the Captain on the phone. Are you out of your mind?" Scott reached for the phone.

Ben slapped his hand down on the receiver to hold it in place. "He's got nothing else to do.. He can chit-chat with you later. This is important."

Trudy tried to step back from the fire flashing in the Lieutenant's eyes but Ben still had her snagged by the wrist.

"Chit chat?" The man slammed his fist on his paper-stacked desk. "You think the captain calls me every day? You think we're swapping *recipes* on the phone?"

"Can it, Scott. This is important."

"Can it? *Can it?* Ben, I ought to..."

"Ralph Watson. You've been after him for years. He lives it up while women get coerced out of filing complaints. We've got a folder on him. He lives in Bourne, flaunts his money and makes a fortune writing books about his abuse of woman. Well, I've got a woman who won't drop the charges this time."

The Lieutenant dropped into his chair. His eyes cut away from Ben and zeroed in on Trudy. "You? You're going to press charges against this guy? I had him cold when I was in uniform. Dragged him off the poor woman myself. We nailed him that time because I was the eye witness. He went away for two years. We managed to hang on to the felony conviction. He's..."

"Yeah, yeah, right, we know all about the bad boy." Ben waved his boss' story aside like it was a pesky gnat. "You want to hear her or what?"

"Garrison," the lieutenant growled. "You've got the people skills of a pit bull."

Ben shook his head. "I pulled him off of her, too. So, she pressing charged and I'm the witness, just like you were. We'll get him again. At first, he claimed he only approached her to talk to her, and that the scrape on her face was her fault for fighting him. She's a bleeding heart and was going to wimp out of it. But now that he's emailing her twenty times a day and..."

"Fifty," Tru interjected.

"She's ready to testify. We can finally nail him on a third strike. He's got a list of priors, all with dropped charges that..." Ben's head turned to face Trudy. "Fifty?"

Trudy nodded. "I got a bunch more last night."

A broad smile broke across Ben's face. "Oh, man that's great."

The lieutenant looked at her with sympathetic eyes. "That's awful, Miss Jennings. You must be upset."

"Well, honestly it's..."

"Sure, it's awful." Ben cut her off and went on with his own yammering. "The worse it gets for her, the better it gets for us. He's really harassing her. Add to that he's hanging around her office and we've got him on stalking..."

"And my home."

"...charges that will add another..." Ben turned to her again and locked his gun-slinger eyes on her, no smile this time. "Your home? He came to your home?"

"Yes." Trudy shrank a little under Ben's dead-eye gaze.

"When?"

"Two nights ago." She'd planned to tell him yesterday, but she'd been so annoyed with him...and this morning, he'd wanted to hear about her work and she'd gotten sidetracked. "He was on the..."

"Did he get inside? You never said anything. I suppose you didn't lock the door. That's so dumb. How can you be so careless?" Ben shook his head. "Somebody oughta lock you up for your own safety. Did he touch you? Did he..."

"Will you shut up?" Trudy shouted.

The room fell silent.

Trudy's cheeks heated. Ben narrowed his eyes at her. The Lieutenant rubbed his hand over his mouth, but Trudy could see him smiling.

"Now then," she said, giving Ben her sweetest smile. "He was on the beach outside my home. I saw him there around two yesterday morning, but I didn't get a good enough look at him to swear to it in court."

"Are you sure you can't finger him? This isn't more of your give-the-clown-a-break-because-his-mommy-didn't-love-him garbage, is it? You're such a wimp, Tru-Blu. If you know it's him..."

"Ben!" Trudy wasn't sure where that voice came from. She would bet her life it'd never come out of her mouth before. She jerked against his iron clad grip on her arm.

Releasing her by opening his hand one finger at a time, he raised one eyebrow. "Go on."

"I can't swear it was him but that is part of what solidified my desire to do something about him. If you'll remember, I agreed file charges last night but couldn't because of another commitment. Then last night, when we suspected he was loitering around the church, that only made me more determined. For him to come to my home was frightening. It's a private beach and all the homes have fences and security gates."

She looked at the Lieutenant, then at Ben. "Assuming it wasn't one of my neighbors out there—and I can't swear it wasn't, but no neighbor has ever trespassed onto my beach before—then the only way for him to have gotten there, assuming my neighbors didn't let him in voluntarily, is by climbing someone's fence and wading in very rough surf and climbing over stretches of rock for a long way. No one has ever been out there before. That tells me he's determined and over the edge."

She shook her head. "So, although I can't testify to that being him, I can testify to him grabbing me and threatening me at the college. He intended to force me to go with him, he said that clearly. That's attempted kidnapping. I tried to get away from him several times and he restrained me each time. If that night had been a one-time incident, I might have accepted his explanations and excuses but, considering the behavior that has followed, I now know I have to take action to protect myself and to protect other women."

There was a prolonged moment of silence.

Ben said at last, "May I talk now?"

Trudy held his gaze without flinching. "If you're going to continue to insult me, the answer is no."

Lieutenant Sheridan coughed behind his hand. Ben turned on him.

"He's making that same sound you kept making in my class on Monday night." Trudy crossed her arms.

Ben ignored his boss, which Trudy couldn't imagine ever doing to *her* boss. "I thought you were supposed to be so easy going."

"Well, I guess I'm surprising both of us, aren't I?"

"I'm trying to save your life. Liz bullies you every day and you do nothing. How come I get all the grief?"

"You asked me to come in here and press charges." A sudden pang hit Trudy low in her stomach. "I thought you were worried about me, but you're just obsessed with getting a criminal, aren't you?"

She squared her shoulders, aware of her wimpy tone. "Forget I said that. Of course, you're just interested in arresting a dangerous man. What other reason could there be?"

She turned to the snickering lieutenant. "Now, how do I swear out a complaint? Do I have to sign a paper, or raise my right hand and actually swear to it, or what?"

Lieutenant Sheridan rose from his chair and extended his hand. "Hello, my name is Scott Sheridan." He took Trudy's hand. His eyes went to her scraped face. "I'm sorry you were hurt, Dr. Jennings."

He was so kind, and the look of regret over her injury was so sincere, Trudy felt her eyes tear up. "Thank you, Lieutenant. It really was a shocking experience."

With his other hand, he cradled both of hers. "Are you all right? Did he hurt you very badly, Trudy?"

She shook her head, speechless from the gentle concern.

"Ben was in here yesterday, talking with me about possible charges we could file against Watson. We've got some paperwork we'll need you to go over and sign. I'd like to take photographs of your injury."

Trudy nodded. "I've got some deep bruises on my upper arms, too, if you want pictures of those."

"You do?" Ben looked as if he wanted to see them right now. "You never told me that."

"Well, I'm telling you now."

"Yes, we'd like those pictures. We have a police woman with forensics, she'll get photos. Thank you. And then we can arrest him. It's really brave of you to come in. This city would be a safer place if all our citizens were so conscientious."

Ben grabbed Trudy by the wrist again and pulled her out of Sheridan's warm grasp. It was only then that she realized she'd been holding hands with the man through his entire speech.

"Let's get on with it, okay? I'll take her statement." Ben dragged her out of the office. Trudy looked behind her to see Sheridan watching them with a strangely satisfied smile on his face, a smile that didn't match the warm sympathy he'd been showing her at all.

Ben took Trudy into a bland room that looked like the interrogation rooms she'd seen on TV. Her stomach dipped slightly, even though she didn't know why Ben needed to question her.

Ben plunked her down in a chair then sat across from her.

She braced herself for him to bring out the rubber hose. Instead, he slid some papers across the table at her.

"Name Trudy Jennings," Ben muttered to himself as he began to fill in blanks on his own forms.

"What is the matter with you?" Trudy laid her hand over his papers. Ben brushed her hand aside.

Trudy slapped it back in place.

He looked up at her, his brow furrowed. "What's your problem?"

"Who are you and what have you done to the bossy, but not insane Detective Garrison?"

"We're wasting time. Get your hand off that." He reached for her hand.

She formed a fist. "Be-e-e-en." She didn't plan on making his name three syllables long, but it worked out that way.

He stopped wrestling her for control of the papers and looked up with an impatient jerk of his head. "What?"

"Why are you acting like this?"

"Acting like what?"

"You mean you're always such a rude, snotty, impatient, disrespectful pig?"

Ben's impatience faded from his eyes, replaced with what looked to Trudy like hurt. "You're supposed to turn the other cheek. I don't think you can call me names and qualify for Saint-Truhood."

Trudy narrowed her eyes at him. "You know, you pull out my theories to use against me as if you believe in them. But you ignore them when they're inconvenient, and laugh at them the rest of the time."

"This is a police station. We don't have a lot of time for social-izing. Did you want me to invite Scott out for a cup of tea before we filed the report?"

"I think you can find some middle ground between 'invite him out for tea' and 'hang up on his boss.'"

"Maybe," Ben shrugged his broad shoulders. "I've never given it much thought."

"It can't be good for your friendships if you treat your fellow officers the way you just treated everyone who made contact with you in that room."

"I wouldn't know," Ben said. "I don't have any friends."

Trudy arched her eyebrows. "There's a shocker."

Ben looked at the door behind him.

Trudy waited for him to have an awakening.

He turned back to her. "They'll be fine. But if you're really wor-ried about me, you can apply all your counseling methods to me."

Ben pulled a pen out of his shirt pocket and clicked it a few times. "How does it work again? It's a really intensive, prolonged period of one-on-one work, showering the patient with love. You want to volunteer to give me the love that I've missed, Tru-Blu?"

She didn't think Ben meant that the way it sounded. "In your dreams, buddy."

"Fine then." He centered the form. "For the record, my folks are great. They just love the stuffing out of me. I think if we try and blame my problems on a bad childhood, they'll really take it hard. So, I'll keep being my own sweet, if somewhat abrasive, self."

"Somewhat abrasive?"

He grinned at her. "And you answer my questions so we can go bust this guy who's stalking you."

"I won't counsel you. But I'd be glad to refer you to my col-league."

"The overworked Dr. Pavil?" Ben stared at the form for a min-ute.

Trudy almost sighed with relief. He was considering it. He was going to let her help him. He was going to invest himself in the class he was taking from her.

Ben looked up at her. "Not a chance."

He went back to studying his report. He glanced up with his

pen poised over the form. "Date of birth?"

Trudy sighed and mentally turned the other cheek. The one still scraped up from her meeting with Watson.

# CHAPTER ELEVEN

BEN TOOK DOWN TRUDY'S INFORMATION and prepared to bicker pleasantly with her all the way to her job.

"Ben, I'm serious about counseling for you. I don't think you're reacting to people in a way that's conducive to good interpersonal relationships. In fact, a growing body of statistical and ethnographic research suggests that many of today's adults have been raised with a lack of caring, prosocial adult role models. They show all the symptoms of..."

"Tru-Blu, I hope you're enjoying the sound of your own voice because I don't understand a word you're saying."

Sweet little Trudy shot fiery arrows at him with her blue eyes. "What I'm trying to say is..."

"Don't start in on all that psychobabble again, Tru. You're giving me a headache."

"What I'm trying to say..."

"Give plain English just one shot." Ben sent his truck up the road toward Bella Vista Christian College, enjoying the pulse of his truck and the pretty, fuming woman beside him.

"Okay, how's this? You're a little old to still be a detective third grade, aren't you?"

"That's a low blow." Ben glanced away from the road to glare at her. "Just because you make a fortune, doesn't mean everybody has to."

"It's not a low blow. It's an observation. Your lieutenant looks younger than you. You hung up on his boss. You yelled at ten people. Your people skills are wretched, and it's costing you money."

"I make plenty of money. And I've got the best arrest record in the precinct. If I get passed over for promotion because I don't know how to play footsie with the brass, then fine. I'll stay a third grade."

Her eyes lit up, and Ben realized he should have played it cool. Instead, he'd just admitted she was right. Good grief, he'd broken under interrogation like a junky who needed a fix.

"What if Tru Intervention could make you more money?"

"That's not the intent of your books, is it? You didn't write them so I could cash in on them."

"You wouldn't be cashing in. You'd be making peace with the world. The new harmony you felt would make everything in your life easier."

"I've told you, turning the other cheek doesn't work for cops. I can't turn the other cheek with a criminal."

Tru seemed to swell up with indignation. Ben wished he could pull over and watch her get all cranky.

"Could you at least try it with people who *aren't* shooting at you?"

If he hadn't been enjoying her temper so much, he might have missed what she said, because he ignored her boring little speeches most of the time. Unfortunately, he'd been listening, and she'd made some sense.

Ben tapped his fist on the steering wheel and clenched his jaw. He might think her ideas were dumb, but he was honest. And he had to admit she was right. "Yeah, I suppose I could try it on people who aren't shooting at me."

"Why did you do that to Scott? We weren't in that big of a hurry. Why didn't you take three seconds with each person who asked you a question? Instead of yelling, just say, 'I'll get right on that as soon as I've taken the statement of this poor victimized woman.'"

"If I stopped every time someone bothered me, I'd never get any work done." Ben flinched. He shouldn't have pulled the phone out of Scott's hand. Good grief, he'd hung up on the captain.

"Ten people. Three seconds each. 'I'm helping this poor victimized woman.' That's thirty seconds of your day. You're going to do all those reports as soon as you can, aren't you?"

"Yeah."

"Then you wouldn't be lying. You wouldn't be playing footsie. You'd just be speaking softly to people you already respect. It's a bad habit to bark at them. Break it."

"They don't care what I act like. They're used to me."

"What's the raise if you get promoted?"

Ben knew exactly how much. He'd been passed over for it often enough.

"Thirty seconds a day of more polite interaction with your colleagues could add up to thousands of dollars a year—if you've *really* got the best arrest record in the precinct."

"I do," Ben growled.

"Then that tiny change in your behavior might be all it would take."

Dead silence fell over the truck. Ben relished it and wished it would last. It was his turn to have some class, though. "I hate admitting I'm wrong."

"Everyone does." Tru used her Soft Answer Voice, letting him off the hook, sparing his pride. It worked, too. He could feel his temper cooling. Which meant she was right, and he was wrong.

"They'll think I'm up to something."

"You could try honesty. You could say, 'I'm taking a class about changing behavior patterns and it makes a lot of sense. I'm going to try and be an easier man to work with.'"

"I'd sound like such a wiener."

Tru shook her head. "Okay, tough guy, how about you wait until someone says, 'what's up with you, Garrison', and you say…" She lowered her voice an octave. "'I've been bitin' your heads off for the last fifteen years. I'm gonna knock it off.' Is that un–weiner-ish enough for you?"

He grinned across the seat at her. She smiled back.

"Except it's been more like eight years."

"Oh, I thought you only served four years, then went straight into the police force."

"I did."

Trudy's brow furrowed but she said nothing while she revised his age downward five years..

"Tell me what's going on in that head."

"Nothing much."

Ben was good at detecting. "How old did you think I was?"

Trudy gave him the worst innocent smile he'd ever seen. "I have no idea your age. It's never come up. What does that have to do with this?"

He wondered just how old she'd guessed he was…and why? Cynicism might be carving lines in his face. He decided he wouldn't push it, it might hurt.

Looking at the traffic, he eased himself off the interstate toward the college. "I might try that second thing. I could pull that off— some of the time."

"You could." Tru had a smug smile on her face.

He had the impulse to wipe it off. A pathetic impulse, he knew. As part of the new Ben Garrison, he controlled himself. "I'll do it. I'll read your books again and try to put the cynicism on hold and give it a try."

Tru rested her hand on his arm. "And I understand how the work you do could make you cynical. I know you're a Christian, Ben. You shF ould pray about it?

Ben snorted as he pulled onto the university grounds. "Sorry. No snorting from now on, either."

"Not even in class?"

Ben was silent for a minute. "I hate to make a promise I can't keep. How about I just promise to do my best?"

Tru nodded as he pulled to a stop in front of her building. "And I'll stick to my guns, and we'll nail Watson before he hurts anybody else."

Ben threw his truck into park and reached his hand across the seat to her. "It's a deal."

She smiled without a hint of a smirk this time and shook his hand. "Are you picking me up tonight?"

"Four-thirty, right?"

"I won't step outside until you're here." She dropped his hand.

He wasn't tired of hanging around her yet, so he said, "If you have methods to make a person more kind and soft spoken, what's say we experiment with me instead of those hard-case lunatics you're working with now?"

"Hard case lunatics?"

"I was thinking of Liz and your secretary, Ethel."

Tru slid off his truck seat, landed, and turned around. He liked the way her eyes glowed.

"Really? You mean it?" Ben got out and came around to face her. He didn't mean it, not really, but he'd do anything to keep her eyes shining like that. "Sure. What are these methods, exactly?"

He'd told her he'd read her books, and he had, but hard core skimming was the only thing that had gotten him through. He waited for her to call him on it.

"Well, it's intensive; we run shifts of counselors one-on-one, twenty-four hours a day. The counselors give constant encouragement, unconditional love and train our patients to react to situations with a soft answer. I'd stay with you as much as possible."

"How're you supposed to do that?" Ben didn't look at her. "We're both at work all day." He couldn't look at her when he was so mesmerized with the thought of spending twenty-four hours a day, seven days a week with the lovely Tru. He resisted banging his head on the truck door to clear his mind.

Tru looked behind her at the Psycho Building as if she were contemplating resigning her job so she could save him from himself.

She looked back with a little furrow of worry between her eyes. "I usually just refer people. Dr. Pavil has a huge staff of counselors, many of them volunteers, who take shifts. They stay almost 24/7 with a new patient. I don't suppose you'd be interested in being referred?"

"I don't suppose I would." Ben braced himself to give her the bad news that he was just kidding anyway. There was nothing wrong with him.

Okay, sure he was a little short tempered. Who wasn't? He'd already decided to be more polite. Surely he wasn't one of those amoral poverty freaks she was talking about. He was a cop for Pete's sake. Nothing immoral about arresting bad guys for a living.

Before he could call the whole crazy thing off, she whispered, "I'm a failure you know."

Shocked, Ben shut up before he could tell her he didn't want her help. "No, you're not."

"Yes, I am. I write all about how to help people, and I get letters all the time from people who love me because I've helped them so much. But I never do anything. You're right about me living in this safe, ivory tower, spouting theories with no idea if they work."

"They work. I think. At least the books sell."

Tru's face clouded up like an approaching storm.

Ben waited for her to lightning all over him.

"They *do* work." Tru's cute little fists clenched and Ben wished her well with this temper tantrum. Bless her heart, she was still sweet, even when she was angry.

"My message is true," she insisted. "How can a fundamental Biblical message as pure as Love Thy Neighbor *not* be true? Of *course* it's true."

Ben held up his hands to ward off the next crack of thunder. "Hey, you're the one who said you're a failure. If you're going to keep changing sides in the argument you don't need me. You can fight with yourself."

Tru deflated and that worried look appeared again.

*I should have let her yell. She needs the outlet.* Ben decided right then he'd let her take all her repressed anger out on him for as long as she needed. It'd be his own personal counseling ministry.

He looked right in those pretty blue eyes. "Tru-Blu, you're not a failure and your theories work. Of course, love should be the answer. But this planet is filled with imperfect people. Not everyone makes the right choice. In a way, we both have the same job."

"We do not." She looked horrified, and that irritated him. "Our jobs are nothing alike."

"You try and reach people with love. I'm there when they don't accept your help. I'm just a little farther down the curve than you are."

"I really do...or rather...Dr. Pavil and others like him really do help people. Even people who are pretty mixed up have responded to my methods."

"I'm sure they do. I've read some of your email. Not just the crazy stuff from Watson. And I've read the testimonies in the back of your books from people who have changed their lives. Why else would I be willing to work with you on my own dumb self?"

"You're not dumb." Tru's eyes sparked with fierce anger, as if she were defending him against someone else's insults instead of his own.

The vulnerable look faded from her eyes, so Ben teased her again, which was safer than pulling her close and hugging her for being in his corner.

"My job wouldn't exist if everyone loved each other." Ben tucked his hands in his pockets to keep them from getting him in real trouble. "A lot of people fall about a million miles short of loving others. So here I am, gainfully employed. Forget about thinking you're a failure."

"I am a failure, Ben. I believe what I write, but I also think God gave me these words because he meant for me to make a difference in the world."

"You do make a difference."

Tru shook her head, looking like a stubborn little mule. A cute, sweet-smelling mule, but still...

"I think God is disappointed in me. He wanted me to do more than just write the books. He wanted me to work with people."

"You work with your students."

"No," Tru crossed her arms. "I mean troubled people. He gave me this ministry, and I've played it safe. I say all the right words, but I don't get my hands dirty. Do you really think God planned for me to make millions of dollars on a message he sent to me? On books I've written using a gift from him?"

*Millions?* Ben gulped. "You've helped more people with those books, and by training counselors than you ever could have working one-on-one with people."

Tru's jaw clenched, and she planted her fists on her hips as she glared at him. "You know what I mean. I could do all that and still help someone."

"Okay, you'll help someone. Me."

"You don't count. You're not crazy enough."

Ben felt ridiculously grateful for that assessment. "Well, there's no reason to jump in at the deep end of the pool first off. We'll figure out how we're going to fix me, and you'll get some experience as a counselor. I might not be crazy, but we can both agree I'm a failure. Way more than you are."

"We'll do it, Ben. But it won't be like a real counseling job for me, because you're already terrific. It'll just be us working together to try and fix a few little quirks that hold you back."

"And maybe, while we're at it, we could work on toughening you up?"

"I don't need to toughen up."

"Liz," Ben said. Nothing more.

Tru shuddered with blatant fear. "Okay, we can work on a few things."

For one shocking moment, Ben considered dragging her into

his arms and giving her a good-bye kiss. He jogged around his truck to prevent that. "I'll see you at four-thirty."

He drove away smiling. He didn't really intend to change much. Oh, it wouldn't hurt him to dredge up a few rusty manners his mama had taught him as a kid. Please, thank you, stuff like that, but otherwise, he was fine.

It wouldn't be hard to be a fixer-upper for Tru-Blu Jennings. He couldn't wait.

# CHAPTER TWELVE

W HEN SHE GOT THROUGH WHIPPING Ben Garrison into shape, she'd know that she'd done the Lord's work. She couldn't wait.

She was going to work on her theories in the real world. She'd finally get a chance to serve God with her hands as well as her words.

She lay awake for long hours that night rehearsing speeches and getting to the bottom of his hostile view of the world.

Then, when her mind started chasing itself in circles, with her scolding Ben then giving him a hug, then jumping away when the hug felt too nice, then scolding him some more, all while he coughed at her, she turned to the state capitals.

Alabama – Montgomery
Alaska – Juneau
Arizona – Phoenix
Arkansas – Little Rock
California – Sacramento

She also memorized a good portion of the book of James, although she found from hard experience that she didn't retain it well after one o'clock in the morning.

"Tru-Blu, you get down here!"

Ben was early.

She glanced at the clock.

Wrong. She was late.

She dragged her sensible, low-heeled, sling-back taupe shoe on her foot, hopping as she tried to move and finish dressing at the same time. Her eyes burned and her head felt like it was wrapped in cotton. She had to get some sleep one of these nights.

"And the next time I get here and find you in the house..."

Liz!

Liz and Ben were together, without a referee!

Trudy bolted out the door, one shoe on, one shoe off.

"I'm ready, Ben," she sang out, trying to maintain her soft answer voice. She had a feeling she would need it this morning.

"And I'd like to know where you get off..." Liz vibrated with anger, which meant her belly fat and extra chins vibrated, too. The woman was in motion everywhere. She jabbed a stout finger under Ben's nose. "...telling me I can't come in here, when it should be clear to a newborn *basset hound* that I've got Tru's permission to be here."

Trudy stumbled slightly on the last five steps and was plunging to her death when she slammed into Ben.

Of course, he caught her, jerked her to her feet, pulled her up against him to steady her and managed to keep yelling at Liz the whole time. Finally, a man who could multi-task just when she needed him least.

"Ben, remember what we talked about last night?" Trudy wriggled out of Ben's grasp and placed herself between the two sparring partners, facing Ben.

Ben didn't even spare her a glance.

Liz put her hand on Trudy's shoulder.

Yelling into Tru's ear, she said, "Don't you defend this arrogant, pushy..."

Ben caught Trudy's other shoulder and held her in place. "Don't shove your boss around like that."

Ben looked at Trudy for the first time, which was amazing considering he'd snagged her off the steps like a pop fly. "I remember exactly what we talked about last night, Tru. We were going to toughen you up. Well, lesson one starts right now. You tell Liz here that you're not going to put up with her rude treatment and insulting remarks anymore, and then I'll toss her out onto that over-fertilized lawn of yours."

"No," Tru shook her head. "We talked about you learning to deal with people more politely."

"That doesn't include a hostile witness during an interrogation."

"I'm not a hostile witness," Liz snapped.

Trudy held up her hands, hoping that was the universal sign for peace, not surrender. "Let me handle this, Bee."

"Who is Bee?"

Trudy flinched. "Liz. I meant Liz. Let me handle this, Liz. Why don't you go ahead and get to work now? Ben's just upset because he's worried about..."

"You're hostile all right." Ben talked right over Tru. "Why is that by the way? This job too tough for you? Maybe you don't think you get paid enough. Maybe you know more about these crank letters and emails than you're telling."

Trudy felt like the filling in an Oreo.

Ben pushed her out of the way. It would have worked if Liz hadn't been pushing in the opposite direction. They were both too busy to notice she wasn't moving.

"Maybe some of these letters are coming from you." Ben leaned over Trudy's head.

She wished she were a foot taller, and, while she was wishing, she might as well wish to be an offensive lineman for the Dallas Cowboys.

"Or maybe you're trying to scare a raise out of Tru by harassing her." Ben's eyes narrowed. "Or maybe you think you could make more as a bull dog than you're making now."

*Low blow.* Tru had noticed Liz's clothing for the day on her flying trip downstairs. She wore a knee length turtle-neck sweater. Beige. It emphasized her rather unfortunate resemblance to a bulldog. She thought a few minutes of intensive counseling right now might be just the thing for Ben. Too bad she was so busy not getting crushed. She wondered how her real-world counseling actually worked. How did you interrupt someone who behaved in a horribly anti-social way and interject your advice? She decided she had to try.

"Could you please let me have some room here?" Trudy spoke into Ben's shirt front. "There's no reason we can't discuss this calmly, like reasonable adults. We don't have to let our tempers have free rein."

*We? Wasn't that how the Queen of England talked? We are not amused.*

"And how do you figure I'm a witness?" Liz barked. "Witness to what? Nothing ever goes on around here."

"You're a witness to the comings and goings of this house. You know who calls, who sends mail. How is it that Tru hasn't gotten a nasty letter for over a month until yesterday? The emails keep flooding in. The calls come to her work, but not home. If this loon is still harassing her in other ways, why did he stop writing?"

Ben must have exhaled, because Trudy had a square inch to move. She twisted around and faced Liz's electrified, ebony black hair and her bared teeth. She regretted changing positions.

"They come here," Liz snarled. "Letters and calls both. I just hang up on the callers and throw the crank letters in the trash."

"What?" Ben went ballistic behind Trudy and she was suddenly glad she couldn't see him. "You get repeated threatening letters and calls to Tru's unlisted phone number and you don't inform the police or even tell your boss, the woman who pays your salary?"

"Liz is right." Trudy wished she could get behind Ben. Sure, he was bossy and ignored her and pushed her around. But he was a cupcake compared to Liz. "I did tell her to throw them away. This is my fault."

"I told her about it." Liz acted as if Trudy hadn't spoken. "How do you think she knows? She wouldn't even know which way was up if I didn't point the direction every morning."

Trudy narrowed her eyes. The ungrateful woman could at least acknowledge that her employer just took the blame for what went on in this house

"She told you to do that a month ago. When the letters kept coming from the same source, you should have fumbled around until you found a light switch in your brain and realized this was something more serious. Then you should have done something about it."

"Ben, calm down."

He ignored her. "Instead, you toss the letters and hang up on the callers. You leave the phone number the same and don't even tell Tru she might be in danger."

"If she's in danger, it's your fault. That man probably just wanted to talk to her. Now you've interfered and made him mad. You probably made him flip out, and she didn't help because Miss Big Shot TV Star Lady here is too selfish to give the poor guy a few minutes of her precious time, and you were too arrogant to let a desperate man have his say."

"I'm not selfish, Liz. I tried to help him." Trudy was dismayed to hear Liz say that about her. "You shouldn't say things like..."

"I saved her life." Ben leaned over until Trudy could see him by her shoulder. "She just stood there and let him drag her off. If I hadn't been there, she'd have been led to the slaughter like some brainless sheep."

"A brainless sheep? There's no need for either of you to call me names."

"She wouldn't get out the door and head in the right direction in the morning if it weren't for me."

Trudy felt a little spit on her face when Liz yelled, "She doesn't have the sense God gave belly button lint. It's a wonder—."

The spit and the insults and maybe the Oreo filling treatment were all too much.

"All...right...knock...it...off!" She couldn't believe she could shout that loud.

Silence fell over the room.

Ben craned his neck and looked down at her. Liz stepped a couple of millimeters away from her. Trudy felt a little light-headed, but good. Very good.

"I'm not going to stand here and be called names by two people whose salary I pay."

"You don't pay my salary, Tru-Blu." Ben rested a hand on her shoulder.

"I'm a taxpayer, so shut up!" She glared up at Ben, surprised to see a rather satisfied smirk on his face.

Liz's fat, grubby hand closed on the shoulder Ben wasn't holding. "You're not going to talk to me like that, you little..."

Tru twirled to face Liz, this time with some room to operate. "You're fired."

"About time." Eleanor stood not two feet away, holding a cast iron skillet, waiting for the go-ahead to bash somebody.

"You can't fire me, I quit." Liz fumbled in her purse and pulled out her cigarettes. "You won't last a day around here without..."

"Fired! Now! Get out!" Trudy thought she'd gotten all her temper out of her system with the one blast. Apparently, she was wrong.

Liz reached out, then glanced over Trudy's shoulder. Trudy didn't know what Liz saw, but she lowered her hand, stuck the cigarette in her mouth, and pulled out a lighter.

Eleanor snatched the lighter away.

"Hey, that's mine."

"Light up when you're on your way out." Eleanor went to the front door and tossed the lighter onto the lawn.

Liz glared, and turned back to Trudy. "The computer's got a password on it. You can't even open it to pay your bills. You can't make your house payment without me. You can't..."

"Eleanor."

"Yes, Trudy?"

"Go try and open the computer. If you can't do it, call in a technician to either open it or block my personal information and start new accounts. Have that include new bank account numbers and any other financial accounts Liz has access too."

Trudy turned back to Liz. "The nice thing about bills, Liz, is they try like the very dickens to collect them. If I don't pay when they first bill me, I promise, they'll try again next month. So, I'll manage just fine alone. You know I lived without you for the first, oh, twenty-six years of my life. How do you suppose I managed that?"

Liz opened her mouth, glanced over Trudy's shoulder, and closed her mouth.

"Have you got any personal possessions in that office?" Trudy asked.

Ben said with quiet menace, "It will be my pleasure to escort you anywhere in the house to pick up your things. But you aren't going to wander around here alone, not even for one split second."

Liz snapped, "You've got nothing here I want."

With enough rage to crack the ceramic tiles in the foyer, she stomped past Trudy and Ben.

Just as she jerked the door open, Liz turned and focused her bulldog eyes on Trudy. She said with acid sweetness, "The password for everything is *doctorwimp101*."

Trudy took a couple of steps past Ben to prove to Liz she didn't intend to back down. When the door slammed, Trudy checked the ridiculous chandelier overhead to see if it would come down on their heads.

And now that she'd handled one obnoxious, insulting person in her life, she had another one to deal with.

She turned on Ben.

He looked up as if he were trying to decide if he needed to get out from under her chandelier.

# CHAPTER THIRTEEN

B EN DECIDED THE THOUSAND OR so light bulbs on the
ceiling were going to hold. He gave Tru a pat on the shoulder.
"I'm really proud of you. My mild mannered little kitten has some
claws after all. Good job booting Liz out the door."

"Get your hand off me."

Ben lifted his hand slowly from her shoulder. Eleanor snickered
but he didn't take his eyes off Hurricane Tru.

"Okay." He'd wanted to toughen her up. But now he felt a
twinge of regret. The kitten had become a tiger, and turned on
him.

"Brainless little sheep?" Tru clenched her teeny soft fists and
took a menacing step toward him.

He wasn't scared.

He leaned over until his nose almost touched hers. "I wondered
how many insults you'd stand there and take before you defended
yourself. I had a list of names to call you as long as my arm."

Brushing one finger down the tip of her nose, he said, "And I
didn't mean any of 'em. I think you're great. One of the smartest,
nicest, bravest ladies I've ever met. Too sweet for your own good
but, trust me on this, I know there are a lot worse things to be."

Biting back a smile, he watched her turmoil rage. She wanted to
tear him limb from limb. Good. His plan was working. Slowly, her
rigid shoulders relaxed and the red in her face lightened. Then she
got all wide-eyed, as if worried about how rude she'd been.

"I told you to shut up."

"You sure did, darlin'." Ben shrugged, proud of her. "And I
deserved it."

"No, you didn't. I'm supposed to be helping you deal with bad situations in a more loving way. And here I've been the worse possible example. My disgraceful behavior this morning may have set your counseling back days or even weeks."

Ben couldn't look away from her. She was all stormy and irritated, with too much color in her cheeks and the blue in her eyes nearly burning him alive. "I'm still improving. Didn't you notice how nice I was to the killer bee?"

"Nice?" Tru screeched. "You were rude. You insulted her and shouted. For heaven's sake, Ben, you called her a bull dog."

"Noticed that, did you?" Ben couldn't hold back a snort of laughter.

Tru's eyes narrowed.

"I know I was rude. But when it was about you, I was teasing. You're such a sweetheart, I just couldn't resist."

"You weren't going to snort anymore, as I recall."

"That's my last one." Ben put his hand over his heart and kept a straight face even though it almost killed him.

Tru shook her head and turned to Eleanor. "What'll we do about covering the phone today?"

Eleanor waved her hands, one holding the skillet, at Trudy. "Go on to work. I'll handle it. And I think I'll hire the next personal assistant, if it's all the same to you."

Tru nodded as if she were exhausted. Ben took a closer look and saw the dark circles under her bloodshot eyes and the slight trembling of her lips. She *was* exhausted. "How much sleep did you get last night?"

Trudy grabbed her purse. "Come on, I'm going to be late to work."

"That much, huh?" Holding her arm, he opened the door, sorry he'd put her through this morning's scene with Liz. He could have waited until she'd had a good night's sleep. "Eleanor, I want this ridiculous door fixed as soon as possible. It ought to be steel reinforced. And change the lock, now that Liz is fired."

Eleanor gave him a sharp little salute. "Yes, sir, we need to keep Trudy safe."

"You're finally growing a spine, Tru. Good girl."

Trudy turned and faced him, uncertain how to right the wrong she'd done to Ben. "What I did today isn't growing a spine. It's losing my temper. I'm not proud of myself."

"Well, I am. I like to see a woman who won't let herself be pushed around. That's great."

He grinned at her like a smug ten-year-old. She had to move fast to repair the damage she'd done. How about if she used blatant manipulation, focusing all her womanly wiles on Ben? That ought to take about three seconds, seeing as how she didn't have a wily bone in her body.

"Okay, I did something you think is great. I learned how to tackle a difficult situation and not wilt in the face of a confrontation. Now it's your turn."

"My turn for what?"

Trudy tried out her very sweetest, manipulative, female smile. "Your turn to try things my way. I'll take a personal day tomorrow. My methods include intensive twenty-four-hour-a-day therapy. My patients are supposed to have someone live with them, correcting old, incorrect responses. I can't come and live with you—" A certain gleam in Ben's eyes told Trudy he planned to say something she'd have to slug him for, so she hurried on. "—but I can spend all day tomorrow with you."

"I don't have a day off. Those pesky criminals don't take annual leave days."

"Pick me up as usual, and I'll go to the office with you. I'll encourage and gently instruct you on how to correct basic, chronic antisocial reflexes as you interact with your peers."

"As I what?"

He was sweet—dumb as a rock—but really sweet. "Let me say it in layman's terms."

"I can live in hope." Ben looked at the roof of his truck.

Or maybe he was praying. Trudy wasn't certain which. "It is critical, as your counselor, that I invest myself through time and effort, in becoming an encouraging, responsible, caring, pro-social adult role model if I hope to effect significant change in your inter-relative responses."

"Do you have any aspirin?" Ben looked like he was contemplating ramming the truck into a cement barricade and sending them flying off the overpass.

If he did, Trudy vowed she'd treat it as a teachable moment and instruct him on more appropriate uses of his energy. "Working with you isn't the same as working with subjects often referred to by criminologist as super-predators. Unlike those born into abject moral poverty."

Ben glanced at her. "I've heard you mention moral poverty before. That means it's a sin to let people be poor, right?"

"Moral poverty is a situation in which there is no underpinning in the rearing of a child regarding basic human decency and a misplaced regard for activities historically considered by the general population as immoral."

Ben's hands clenched the steering wheel until his knuckles turned white. "I am *begging* you to speak English."

"What I mean is," she said with exaggerated patience. "I'm going to hang around you every minute and, every time you're rude, I'm going to give you a swift kick in your backside."

Ben relaxed. "Oh. Okay. That I understand."

He sat up straight and glanced at her. "Except, uh...no, you're not. I don't think you'd better come into the station with me. The precinct house is no place for a civilian, unless they're under arrest, of course."

"Of course." Trudy smiled. "I fired Liz. I let you manipulate me into being tough with her. You owe me."

"How does your dumping the two-legged bulldog mean I owe you?" Ben wheeled his truck, like a black bullet, off the interstate.

Trudy looked for a posted speed limit sign without success. Ben was driving unusually fast. Probably anxious to get rid of her. "I believe I explained this earlier."

Ben shrugged. "You might have, but you were speaking psycho-ese, so it's hard to be sure."

"Psycho-ese? That would be...?"

"Doctor talk." Ben shrugged. "A psychologist's version of the language regular doctors use to keep you so off balance that when you leave their office, you realize you forgot to tell them there's a bone sticking out of your leg."

"Psycho-ese," Trudy muttered. She settled in her seat so firmly, it would take dynamite to blast her out. "I'll expect you Monday morning at eight-thirty."

"Expect away. You're not coming to work with me."

A tense silence reigned as Ben drove on to Trudy's building. When he pulled to a stop, she swung the door open. "If you don't come, I'll come to you."

Ben narrowed his eyes like an old west gunslinger at high noon.

"That's right, Ben." She gave him her sweetest smile—except maybe she bared her teeth too much. "I'll wander all around, with no bodyguard, risking life and limb to find you."

She saw his jaw popping and fluttered her eyes at him, trying to use her womanly wiles. They seemed rusty at the moment.

*Oh, forget the wiles.* She'd use the technique of her most difficult pupil. She slid out of the truck, face straight, eyes hard. "Eight-thirty. Don't keep me waiting."

She marched off toward the Psych building so he wouldn't see the smug smile on her face. She might have just won her first round in what seemed to be a never-ending battle with Detective Garrison.

Ben dusted the monitor of his computer for the third time.

"Garrison!" Scott stuck his head out of the door and shouted louder than was necessary, even in the noisy police station. "I should have had your report on my desk forty-eight hours ago."

Scott marched toward him. Ben opened his mouth to snarl back and thought of running to pick Tru up in a few minutes. He could dust all he wanted but that wasn't what she cared about.

He gritted his teeth and reached for a file he'd let sink to the bottom of his 'out' box. He picked it up and turned as Scott bore down on him, eyes blazing.

"Here it is, Scott." Ben forced his face into a smile when he wanted to throw the report, all fifteen unstapled pages of it, in Scott's face. Instead, he extended the forms politely and told the truth. "I finished it up when I first came in at six this morning. I got sidetracked when that double murder came in and forgot to deliver it to you. I apologize."

Scott, reaching for the form, snatched his hand back. "What'd you do, put a bomb in the report?"

Ben clenched his jaw. He'd grind his teeth down to nubs before he'd tell Scott to take a flying leap. He was turning over a new leaf after all.

"You want the report or not?" *Okay, that wasn't a soft answer.* He scrambled for something else to say. Something that wasn't so phony his boss would report him to Internal Affairs, or so sweet the whole stationhouse would need an insulin shot. He came up blank.

The rudeness must have reassured Scott because he took the report and, extending it as far from his body as his arms would reach, he flicked the file open. When it didn't blow, he pulled the paperwork close, studied it a second, and nodded. "Thanks for this, man. I know you've been swamped."

Scott turned and strode back into his office.

Ben sank into his chair, shocked. "What do you know, it works."

"Garrison!" Detective Daisy Yarrow, a heavy-set black woman that had been carping at everyone in the department since before there *was* a department, waved an empty coffee pot in the air like it was the starting flag at a demo derby.

"You took the last cup of coffee, you worthless, lazy, sludge-sucking cockroach. How many times have I told you how things work around this dump?"

*Maybe ten thousand times?* She crabbed at anyone who didn't make coffee. She crabbed at anyone who did make coffee because the coffee tasted awful. That made it easier to just let her do it and take his turn in the getting-yelled-at rotation.

Instead of yelling back like he usually would, he smiled and sweetly said, "Make your own coffee, Yarrow."

Yarrow yammered at him some more.

Ben told her to shut up but he did it quietly, then he ignored her while she yapped some more. He didn't want her distracting him from all he'd learned about using a soft answer to turn away wrath.

He smiled as he pulled the next file toward him. He had to get Tru in about thirty minutes and he didn't want any sign of a crime anywhere near her. Tru wouldn't be able to believe it when she saw him in action.

He'd become a gentleman with the manners of an angel.

Ben had the manners of a pig.

Trudy couldn't believe it when she saw him in action.

"And then we enter all the data into the computer so it's

accessible." Ben hovered behind her while she sat in front of the computer. He'd spent his morning giving her a guided tour of the police station, which was fine, very interesting, perfect for third graders on a school field trip. Except...

"Did you drain this pot again, Garrison?" A woman wielded a coffee pot as if it were a deadly weapon. "I've about had it with you. Why is it always my job to take care of things like this? You left a mess in the break room, too. I'm not your mama. I'm not going to clean up after you for the rest of your life. One of these days I'm gonna..."

Trudy's mouth fell open at the woman's manner.

"Beat it, Yarrow." Ben straightened from where he'd hovered by Trudy ever since he'd plunked her in his chair and spent the morning telling her about police procedure as if this was 'Take your Therapist to Work Day'.

"Go nag your husband for a change and get off my back. I don't have time to..."

"Ben!" Trudy rose from her chair and planted herself directly between Ben and the lady swinging the coffee pot. For a second, it reminded her of the morning with Liz and Ben, except this lady was armed. She had a coffee pot...and a gun.

Trudy faced Ben. If she got whacked with the pot, at least she wouldn't have to see it coming. Besides, Ben was her patient. Maybe she should sign Miss Yarrow up for a course later. Assuming Trudy lived through the day.

Ben looked away from Yarrow and grinned at Trudy. "What?"

"Try again." Trudy waited.

"Try what?" He had a look of such confusion on his face, Trudy considered giving up on writing and teaching. Maybe she'd move to a nice quiet convent somewhere, one where she had to take a vow of silence. She might as well because, so far, everything she'd said and done with Ben had made absolutely zero impact on him.

She leaned close enough so poor Miss Yarrow wouldn't hear. Then maybe the woman would think the new polite Ben was his own idea. "Try responding to her again. This time, use a soft answer."

Ben shook his head, his brow furrowed, and whispered back, "But the only soft answer she wants is for me to say I'll make the coffee. I don't make coffee."

"Why not?"

"Uh...'cuz I don't want to?" Ben looked at her as if she were stupid.

For a woman with a doctorate, the youngest tenured professor in the history of Bella Vista Christian College, and a best-selling author, being thought of as dumb was an experience so unique, she almost enjoyed it. A whole blonde side of herself seemed to blossom when Ben looked at her like that.

Still, she was going to have to kill him.

"Do it, Ben." Trudy did her best to channel authority and domination. "Be nice."

Ben grinned at her. "My coffee stinks. We'll have a riot on our hands if I make it."

"If you refuse to make new coffee, then you shouldn't take the last cup."

Beside them, Yarrow said, "Garrison, quit flirting with your girlfriend and get in there and refill this pot."

Trudy frowned and turned.

Ben caught her by the shoulders and whispered in her ear, "Don't say anything you'll regret."

Yarrow stood a couple of feet away from them, looking like she might empty the bitter black dregs in the bottom of the pot over Ben's head. Ben definitely wasn't the only one in this building with inter-relative issues.

Trudy backed up a step as Yarrow advanced on them. "Do it, Ben. Offer to make the coffee."

"Can't." Ben held Trudy in place when she tried to slide sideways away from the coffee pot wielder. Suddenly his grip wasn't supportive. He was using her as a human shield.

"She'll kill me," he whispered in Trudy's ear. "She'd see it as weakness and go after me like a shark after blood."

"Do it," Trudy said over her shoulder. "You offer to make the coffee right now, or I'm bringing Liz, Ethel and Ralph over for dinner tonight for group therapy sessions."

Ben's hands dug into her shoulders. After a long second, he hissed into her hair, "Fine. But I'm going to make you drink a cup of my coffee."

"Fine," Trudy snipped back.

He let go. "You're absolutely right, Yarrow, uh...I mean Daisy."

Trudy looked at the woman, big enough to play center for the Cowboys, and wondered what had possessed her mother to name her Daisy. The poor policewoman had to have weighed twenty pounds at birth. On the other hand, she'd make a great back-up if a fellow cop were arresting someone.

Yarrow's eyes narrowed. "What are you up to, Garrison?"

The pot seemed to quaver as if Daisy kept herself from hurling it at Ben's head by sheer will power.

"I'm up to nothing. You're always carping..."

Trudy reached behind her and sank her claws into Ben's arms. Too bad for him, he'd taken off his suit coat and rolled up his sleeves.

# CHAPTER FOURTEEN

"OUCH." BEN JERKED HIS ARM free. "Uh...what I mean is you've reminded me of the rules. I'll admit I don't take my turn, and that's going to end. I'll never leave the coffee pot empty again."

Out of the corner of her eye, Trudy saw Ben raise his right hand, as if being sworn in for a trial. "So help me, uh...well, that is, I just promise."

Ben stepped up beside Trudy. "And Daisy, this isn't my girl-friend."

The carafe jabbed forward. "Call me Yarrow, or you're gonna be swallowing this pot in one bite."

Trudy thought Ben might know full well Daisy didn't like her name and used it to undo his gallantry, hoping Trudy wouldn't catch on. If that was the case, then he was a rat fink and Trudy would have to claw him again. She polished her nails against the front of her shirt.

"I'm just trying to help this poor, victimized woman."

Trudy heard the exact words she'd told Ben to say coming out of his mouth. They didn't sound half bad. He might have overacted a little on the poor-victimized-woman line, but it might not be the actor, it might be the lines. After all, she wasn't a playwright.

"She's being stalked by a rich idiot with a good lawyer."

Daisy Yarrow's eyes softened. She lowered the pot. "A man is after you, huh?"

Trudy nodded.

Daisy reached out and ran one finger, surprisingly gentle for a potential line backer, down Trudy's scraped cheek. "He do this to you, honey?"

Moved by Daisy's maternal concern, Trudy couldn't talk. She just nodded again.

"It's not over," Ben said. "He dodged the search warrant, but we arrested him and are hoping the judge binds him over for trial."

Trudy forgot all about play acting in the face of Yarrow's kindness. She got a little teary. "He's already got two felony convictions for hitting women, but the judge wasn't allowed to consider that for some reason."

"Three strikes, huh?" Yarrow studied Trudy's face a moment longer, crossed her arms, and looked up at Ben. "You can introduce criminal history if you're going for a third felony. How'd he dodge the search warrant?"

All of a sudden, Ben wasn't being polite or rude, and neither was Yarrow. They were just being cops. Trudy had a moment to consider that probably neither of them took the whole coffee issue very seriously.

"His lawyer's slick."

"Which judge?"

"Patinkin."

Yarrow snorted. "I coulda guessed. You should've got your mom. She'd've nailed him."

"I really will start making coffee, Yarrow," Ben said. "I just got so much guff because my coffee's so bad, that I quit."

"Yeah, right, like anybody else's coffee's any good."

"Yours is the best. That's why we all stick you with it."

"I know." Yarrow turned, pot still in hand.

Trudy reached out and caught Yarrow's shoulder. "I'll teach him how to make it right."

Daisy turned and her sharp cop eyes studied Trudy for a minute, then with a huge smile handed over the pot. "Good luck with that."

She looked past Trudy to Ben. "You sure she's not your girlfriend?"

Ben stepped up beside Trudy and grinned in a way that made Trudy's heart flip flop like a politician during election season.

"Nah, she's way out of my league."

"Who isn't?" Yarrow smirked and shook her head of tight black curls.

"Good point. No, I'm trying to keep her safe until we get this jerk who's bothering her. She had the day off, so she came into work with me. She's trying to improve me, teach me how to watch my mouth. She's a psychologist who specializes in people with amoral travesty. She's doctoring me."

"Moral poverty," Trudy interjected. "And he isn't my patient."

"Sure I am."

Trudy pivoted and faced Ben. "I'm not your doctor. Don't say that."

"Why not?"

Trudy started to answer and that left her with her mouth hanging open because she realized she couldn't say the answer out loud. She couldn't be Ben's doctor because doctors can't get involved with their patients, and she had just now realized that she was, ever so slightly, involved with Ben Garrison.

"You've never paid me so I'm not your doctor. I'm just a friend helping you out. Okay?" She clamped her mouth shut.

"You want me to pay you? I never thought of that. What do you charge?"

"I don't want you to pay me. I just said I didn't."

"Okay." He shrugged.

The way he did it told Trudy that he'd never considered the ramifications of a doctor-patient relationship being a problem. Which meant he'd never considered her in any way that was personal. Her stomach sank and she fixed her eyes firmly on the floor, not wanting either of these astute students of human nature to see how upset she was.

Trudy needed to grow a brain back since hers had abandoned her. She wasn't interested in any man, anyway. She already failed God by writing and teaching when she should be helping people personally. She couldn't take on more distractions until she got her spiritual house in order.

"She's not my doctor. She's just a nag."

Trudy elbowed him. Yarrow laughed.

"Give me the pot, and I'll put some coffee on." Ben reached out. Trudy handed it over.

Ten detectives hooted and yelled insults at Ben.

"We'll die if he's in charge of coffee."

"Just shoot me now." A piece of wadded up paper sailed past

them.

One officer pulled his handcuffs off his belt and threatened to arrest Ben if he went near the break room.

Minding your manners with this crowd might be a little harder than Trudy had imagined.

Ben slammed his fist on Scott's desk. "How am I supposed to tell her this?"

Scott, his ebony skin gleaming under the florescent light of his office, vibrated with anger as he grabbed the sheet of paper out of Ben's hand. "The judge made his ruling. There's nothing we can do about it."

"He left marks on her. Bruises on her arms and that scrape on her face. That's assault anywhere on this *planet*."

"Watson has a top-notch lawyer. He spun the story to the judge just the way he did to you that first night. You know Trudy believed it at first. Why wouldn't the judge?"

"Trudy never believed it. She knew the guy was a nut job. She's just a bleeding heart. She wants to save the world."

Scott shrugged. "You just described Patinkin."

"Watson has priors."

"The judge refused to admit them as corroborating evidence. All the charges were dropped."

Ben gritted his teeth. "We land felonies on people for less than this every day."

"Not rich people."

"Rich man's justice." Ben grabbed the phone off the hook, then snapped it back in the cradle. "If you can afford a good enough lawyer, the law doesn't apply to you."

"You've got to tell her."

"She's going to have to hire a bodyguard."

"That's the way it works. When the going gets tough, the rich hire bodyguards."

"That wacko is going to keep coming. He'll be even more brazen now that he got off."

"We did come away with a restraining order. If he approaches her again, we can take it back to the judge."

"Great, so Trudy gets a piece of paper to protect her. Maybe she can roll it up and whack him with it next time he attacks."

"Where's she going to get a bodyguard?"

Ben looked up from his desk and thought he caught a faint twist to Scott's lips. "Is anything about this funny?"

Scott raised both hands in front of him. "Not a thing. Don't start in on me."

Ben narrowed his eyes at Scott's feigned innocence and waited for the next crack.

"You know, I really like that woman." Scott looked open, honest and sincere, so Ben knew he was up to something. "She's a sweetheart. Brave and beautiful, too. I think she kind of liked me. Not like you, she was always fighting with you about something. But you have no finesse, Garrison. Me? I'm oozing with charm."

"You want to see something ooze?" Ben threatened.

Scott's smile grew. "I thought she had you working on your people skills. Comments like that are the reason you're still a detective sergeant and I'm a high and mighty lieutenant. I know how to work and play well with others."

Scott was teasing him, but they'd been over this ground before. Scott was right. Ben had gotten so cynical that he couldn't even pretend to play the political games necessary to get ahead on the force.

Ben could have lived with that. He hated office politics. But it went deeper than that. Ben had forgotten how to be a good friend. And he'd forgotten how important a kind word was to an exhausted fellow officer.

But since he'd been spending time with Tru and all her warm and fuzzy ideas, he'd become sensitized for the first time in years.

It was a real pain in the neck.

Scott didn't let him dwell on the dead end of his career. He threw another punch. "You think a classy dame like that'd go for a lowly cop? I could play bodyguard. She'd be so grateful she might..."

"Shut up, Sheridan." Ben lifted the phone again, then hung it up. "I'd better drive over to the campus. She needs to hear this from me in person."

The cheesy grin faded from Scott's face. "Sorry you've got to be the one to tell her."

"What I'm sorry about," Ben said, "is that I'm condemning her to a life of fear."

"The way the judge left it, there's only one way we're going to get this guy." Scott stacked things on his desk with sharp precise movements, which Ben had seen him do a million times when he was unhappy with a case.

"Yeah." Ben snagged his sports coat off the back of his chair as he stood. "Watson is going to have to do something bad to her."

As Ben left the station, he knew telling Tru wasn't the bad part. The prisoner would go free and Tru-Blu would find herself in prison.

# CHAPTER FIFTEEN

"IT'LL BE LIKE I'M LOCKED up in prison." Trudy sank into her office chair, dismayed at Ben's news.

"It's no problem for me to pick you up and drop you off every day. Once Eleanor gets that new front door, your house will be secured." Ben stood in her office, early for class, and prepared to drive her home afterward, just as he had for the past three weeks.

"And at work, you're just going to have to stay in this building."

"Oh, great. It's not prison. It's house arrest with a work release program." Trudy thought about that night when she'd seen a man on her beach. Was it him? There was no proof, and the judge hadn't believed her.

*Secured?* Right. What good was house arrest if the bad guys could walk right up to her back door?

She spun her computer screen around so Ben could get a good look.

His eyes narrowed as he studied her email listings. "How many, today?"

"I don't count anymore. You want me to keep forwarding them to you?" She closed her email and opened it again. Three more messages ticked onto the screen.

"Keep putting them in the file you created. He might change the message and write something incriminating."

"And the restraining order can't do anything about it, right?" Trudy's stomach sank as, *'Give me what I want, or I'll take it'* popped up on her subject line again. Each of them came from a different sender. They popped onto the screen like an army of invading ants crawling down her monitor and up her spine.

"Watson denies he's sending them." Ben ran a hand through his unruly brown hair. "There's no way to prove him wrong."

Trudy rested one elbow on her desk and sank her chin into her hand. "Turn the other cheek," she muttered.

"You know, you mutter that every time you're upset." Ben tilted his head. "I think that makes it a mantra. Isn't that kind of…I don't know…Hindu or something?"

Trudy managed her first real smile since Ben had dropped her off this morning. She looked away from her computer screen to a pile of unopened letters, knowing she'd have just as many at home tonight, since Liz wasn't throwing them out. And the hang-up calls never ended here or at home. Since the number was always different, it couldn't be blocked, so the phone rang constantly.

"It's a wonder this guy has the time to write his books." She pointed to the stack of thrillers on the corner of her desk.

Ben picked up a book and studied it. "Why don't you get rid of them? Even if reading them teaches you something about what makes this guy tick, it doesn't make any difference. Bottom line, he's a loon. Reading those books just fills your brain with sludge."

"They're awful, aren't they? All the violence, especially toward women, all the graphic, loveless sex. I can hear Ralph speaking out of the pages of this book, telling me how he views the world."

"Yeah, I heard they're making a movie out of the first one."

Trudy growled. "Great, that means he's got even more money, which makes him more sure he's the center of the universe. And that means he'll never face his problems and get help."

"Well, we wouldn't want poor Ralph to go without help."

Trudy shrugged. "Unless he gets help, he'll never believe he's doing anything wrong by pestering me."

"It's stalking, Tru, not *pestering*. Pestering is what a two-year-old does who wants something from the candy aisle at the store. This is a little more serious than that."

"I know it's serious," Trudy snapped. She froze, then slipped her hand over her mouth and gave Ben a wide-eyed look of apology. "I'm sorry."

Ben smiled. "Me, you got no problem giving a hard time. But, *Ralph*, you worry about."

"I'm failing." Trudy's eyes clouded up. She blinked to keep the tears from falling. "The first real test I've ever had, to remain true to my convictions, the convictions I've been spouting..." Her voice broke.

"No, please, don't cry." Ben groaned and fished in his pocket for a handkerchief.

She took it and dabbed under her eyes, mindful of her make-up and the approaching class and her failure.

Trudy flipped a paper over on her podium as she made her closing point for the night's class.

"The psychology of turning the other cheek has long been recognized. In a study done by the Institute for..."

A gangly boy stood from his desk and slapped himself on the back side. "Turn this cheek, baby."

The class broke into smothered giggles as the troublemaker plopped back in his chair.

Trudy was used to the high spirits that followed a big test.

Ben glared at the mouthy kid until the room fell silent and the kid almost slid under his desk.

After class, Trudy and Ben stood alone in the room. "You can't use your police tactics on my students, Ben."

"Sure I can. I just did."

Trudy snapped the latches on her briefcase. "He was just voicing his opinion. It's my job to reply in a way that demonstrates my methods. I have to give him a soft answer. If he's determined to be unkind, I have to turn the other cheek. It's what we've been working on together."

"Tru-Blu, you can't run a class without discipline."

"Stop calling me that." Trudy flinched. She slapped her hand over her mouth and looked up at Ben.

Ben let his head droop as if he was too exhausted to hold it up.

"Ben," Trudy said from behind her fingers. "I don't know why I do that to you."

Ben looked up at her and smirked. "Gotcha."

Trudy swatted him on the arm and stormed out of the room.

Ben caught her before she could get outside. "Tru, how many times do I have to tell you to let me go first?"

A cold shiver raced up Trudy's spine. She lagged back and let Ben go ahead.

Ralph Watson stood ten feet in front of the door, his hands in his back pockets, and a contrite look on his face.

Ben reached for his handcuffs. "Watson, you've been informed that you have to stay away from Dr. Jennings."

"I know." Watson just stood there. Silent. Sad.

Ben approached him and grabbed him by the shoulder. "You're in violation of your court order. That gives me the right to arrest you. And this time they can hold you. You have the right to remain silent."

"No, I'm afraid they can't hold him, Garrison." Another person stepped up beside Watson. Trudy hadn't noticed him until he moved. "I am accompanying Mr. Watson. As an officer of the court, that makes this a supervised visitation. The court order allows that."

Trudy recognized Watson's lawyer. Harold Merrick had argued Watson's case at the preliminary hearing and Watson hadn't been required to attend. Trudy had been required to show up, though.

"Merrick, what do you want? You're impeding Dr. Jennings. She hasn't agreed to any visitation and supervised visitation requires her consent." Ben stood so his big body blocked Trudy from both men.

On her tiptoes, Trudy peaked over Ben's shoulder. Ralph was dressed well, clean, his hair trimmed. She saw no aggressive, threatening behavior in body language or his expression. He seemed to be a changed man, or maybe better to say he seemed to be more the man she'd first met.

"I just wanted to tell Trudy that I'll never bother her again. I don't know how things got so out of control. It was never my intention to harm her. All those things you said I did, the emails, the calls, the letters, hanging around your house, that wasn't me. I just wanted to make absolutely sure that you know I'm staying away. If someone is really doing those things, then you need to look for someone else."

Watson looked up from his contrite study of the ground long enough to stare into Trudy's eyes. "I'm worried about you, Trudy. As long as you're blaming me, you're in danger."

Watson turned on his heels and headed across the parking lot. He climbed into the passenger's side of a dark blue Lincoln and sat there, staring straight forward.

"For what it's worth, Ben," Merrick, a stout, expensively dressed man with ruthless eyes, said, "I believe him. If he's not stalking her, then there's someone still out there. Don't spend your time watching out for Ralph and miss the real danger."

On that grim note, Merrick went to his car and drove away.

Trudy came up beside Ben. She watched the car all the way out of the parking lot, and turned to Ben. He studied her with his neutral cop's eyes.

"He sounded sincere." Trudy bit her lower lip as she considered who else might be haunting her.

"He's good. It's no wonder the judge believed him." Ben rested a hand on Trudy's upper arm and escorted her to his truck. He clicked the lock with his remote and opened the door.

Trudy hoisted herself up into the truck quickly so Ben wouldn't give her a boost. She was getting good at scaling the pick-up. Once in, she turned to Ben. "How can you be sure, Ben? He might be telling the truth."

"Because I'm a cop. I've got a nose for liars. And Watson stinks. But it doesn't matter."

Trudy felt her eyebrows arch nearly to her hairline. "Why doesn't it matter?"

"'Cuz I'm gonna be around to save you from Watson. I'll save you from anybody else while I'm at it." He smiled at her and she couldn't help but smile back.

Her smile faded when she thought about what Watson had said. "Ben, is it possible that I overreacted? The man could be completely innocent."

"I told you, he's not." Ben rounded the truck and got in. He stuck his key in the ignition.

"Yes, I know. Your nose never lies."

"Tru-Blu, I'm an expert, a human lie detector"

Trudy didn't mean to snort when she laughed. "Whatever, I'm starting to feel weird about the restraining order."

"What about on your beach? What about at work the day after he attacked you? What about before he attacked you? You said he asked for your help face to face once before? What about those rustling bushes at your church? What about all those..."

"I mean," Trudy said, touching his arm. "He's never approached me, except that one time that we know of, in a way that's anything but perfectly proper."

"Sneaking along the coast to your beach is proper?"

"We don't know it was him."

Ben cranked the key and the engine roared to life. "It was him, Tru-Blu. Now I'm detecting lies from you. Why do you want to lie for this loser? You read his books. You can see he's a freak."

"I've read Stephen King, but I don't think he can raise pets from the dead. Writers have an imagination, you know."

"None I've ever met." Ben threw the truck into gear and, for a policeman, sworn to uphold the law, he shoved his foot on the accelerator awfully hard.

When the tires quit squalling, Trudy snapped, "What's that supposed to mean?"

"It means I don't know why you can't imagine what would have happened to you if I hadn't pulled that guy off you in the parking lot. It means you're afraid to ever go to your church alone again at night, and you're looking out your bedroom window a hundred times a night while you lie there awake, *but for no reason you can imagine.*"

Trudy muttered through her clenched jaw. "Soft answer, soft answer, soft answer."

"You're doing that Hindu thing again."

"It's not Hindu to meditate on peaceful things." Trudy crossed her arms and stared straight ahead.

Except for the jackrabbit start, Ben didn't break any laws. If he had, she'd have called the police on her cell phone—assuming he didn't take it away from her.

In the chilly silence, they neared her home. "I'm driving myself to work from now on. Don't bother picking me up Monday."

"I'll be here at eight and you'd better not keep me waiting."

Trudy refused to look at him.

He tapped the new entrance code to her driveway, changed since Liz had left.

"Watson seemed to understand the seriousness of the charges against him. I don't think he'll bother me again." She turned in her seat as he pulled to a stop. "So that only leaves you."

"That whole *turn the other cheek* thing is only as good as your mood, isn't it?"

Guilt welled up in Trudy. She started to apologize, but she caught a glint of something calculating in his blue eyes and stiffened her spine. "Okay, pal, here's a soft answer." She leaned close to him and whispered, "Leave me alone. If you show up here to drive me, I'll call the police and get a restraining order for *you*."

She wrenched the door open and slid to the ground. Before she got to her front steps, Ben was beside her.

"Listen, Tru-Blu. I'm not going to let you go off by yourself. Watson is probably..."

"You don't know for sure it's him, so quit acting like you know *anything* about this case." Trudy's voice rose as her confusion and fear swirled around. "For all you know there's someone else out there who's just an email freak. He could be perfectly harmless. The guy on my beach could be someone out walking. Those bushes at church could have rustled in the wind. You found a guy you want to pin all this on and, when he starts to look innocent, you give me a bunch of garbage about a human lie detector."

"Tru, I was trying to lighten things up. But I am a good judge of liars."

"So am I. I'm a trained counselor."

"Who's never practiced on human beings."

Trudy whirled away.

Ben grabbed her by the arm. "Tru, you're overreacting." He pulled her around to face him. "Watson upset you more than you realize and you're taking it out on me because you know I'm safe. Calm down. If you want me to look for another guy, I'll do it. But I'm not letting you go unescorted anywhere until..."

"Not *letting* me? Oh yeah," Trudy jerked against his hold. "I forgot about that house arrest, work release thing."

"It's not house arrest." Ben's voice softened and his grip, though still solid, eased on her arm. "It's just me wanting to make sure you're safe. Is that so bad?"

Trudy looked into his eyes, dark in the muted street lights. They seemed to be boring into her brain, drilling past her resistance, searching for agreement.

"Ben, I...I don't know what came over me. I'm never so rude. I...I didn't mean...you've been so kind."

"So you'll let me drive you to work?"

Trudy looked up at him. He was too close. She couldn't resist that strong will when he was so close. "I'll be here."

Ben nodded. "Thank you, Tru. For now, let me keep you safe."

He released his grip on her arm, but his hand stayed near. He walked her to the door and stayed by her side until Eleanor came out to meet them.

"We've got trouble." Eleanor looked at Ben.

Trudy wondered who Eleanor thought she reported to these days.

# CHAPTER SIXTEEN

BEN WAS GLAD AT LEAST Eleanor reported trouble to him.
"What's wrong? Is it Watson?"

"Worse."

"What could be worse than Watson?" Ben's mind boggled.

"Liz."

Eleanor held out a sheaf of papers. "I tried to pay the bills today and found out all the accounts are empty. I checked old bank statements and found this."

"She's been stealing from me?"

Eleanor snorted. Ben wondered why Tru had that 'snorty' effect on people.

"Not exactly, more like she's been spending your money like a drunken sailor."

Tru shook her head. "I haven't had any large purchases lately."

"That turtle neck sweater you're wearing is a Vera Wang original."

"Vera who?"

Ben looked at Tru's knit top. He had a couple of them that looked similar. He'd gotten them for ten dollars at Wal-Mart. Still, women's clothes were always overpriced.

"It cost eighteen hundred and fifty dollars."

Tru inhaled so sharply she started coughing. Ben whacked her on the back half-heartedly, busy trying to breathe himself.

"Eighteen hundred and fifty dollars?" Tru gasped. "For a shirt?"

"You're shoes are Jimmy Choo." Eleanor pointed at Tru's beige heels.

Tru patted her chest. "And that's somebody important?"

"Four thousand dollars a pair important, Trudy. And you've got fifty pairs of shoes that all cost at least that much. Liz bought them for you."

"No, I don't. There aren't fifty pairs."

"I found them in the storeroom on the third floor."

Trudy shook her head. "I told her my sizes and where I got them. I just assumed she'd reordered from the same place."

"The blazer and slacks are Versace."

"I saw that label, but those things don't have to cost a fortune off the rack."

"Originals, ordered from Milan. Nine thousand dollars. Each. And you've got a closet full of them."

Tru squeaked.

Eleanor pointed over their heads.

Ben looked up at the chandelier sparkling down at him.

Like someone asking for whom the bell tolls, Eleanor said, "Eighty-five thousand dollars."

Tru started sinking. Ben caught her around the waist.

Stiffening her knees, Tru asked, "How much has she spent?"

"She was here a little over six months. She went through over two million dollars."

Ben caught her again.

"Do I have two million dollars?"

Eleanor shook her head. "No. A whole lot of it was bought using credit cards she opened in your name. She's got the credit limit up to fifty thousand dollars and I've found eight different cards. She's been paying the minimum every month. Liz put the minimum down payment on your house but it still took nearly all your cash. Then she started selling your stocks. When those were gone, she borrowed every cent from your IRA and you're going to pay a nasty penalty if you don't replace it. And when that was gone, she started with the cards."

"What else?" Tru whispered, leaning against Ben.

"The pretty blown glass vases in the living room are Chihuly."

"Who?"

"She had the yard re-sodded."

"I told her we didn't really need to do that."

"And a new underground sprinkler system installed."

"The old one was perfectly good."

The plump housekeeper lifted one piece of paper after another. "She had the sand on your beach sifted."

"Sifted? For what?" Tru looked up at Ben.

As if he'd know what you sifted sand for. He didn't have a clue.

Eleanor looked up from her stack. "How should I know?"

"Can you really have your beach sifted?" Ben asked.

Trudy snapped, "How should I know?"

"You've got royalty checks coming in all the time. But you're going to have to do some scrambling to make your house payment."

Ben made sure Tru was balanced on her own feet before he reached past her for the bills. "How carefully have you checked these out, Eleanor? Was Liz skimming? Is she guilty of a crime? I think we should arrest her just on principle. It oughta be illegal to spend eighteen hundred dollars on a shirt. For that matter, it oughta be illegal to *charge* eighteen hundred dollars for a shirt. I may go arrest Vera Wang."

He studied the pile of outrageously overpriced stuff, jewelry, watches, mounds of clothes and shoes, belts and purses, home décor that belonged at a flea market as far as Ben was concerned.

He glanced at Tru. He knew she looked expensive, but he had no idea that if someone stole one of her earrings, they'd be guilty of a felony.

"How soon until that new book is done?" Eleanor asked. "You get another third of your payment when the manuscript arrives at the publishers, right?"

Ben scowled at the bills, placed them on the desk, and looked at Eleanor. "How tough is it going to be for her to make the house payment?"

Tru shook her head, her eyes on at her shirt. Then suddenly she headed up her stairs. "I've got stuff I've never opened. We'll return it."

"I don't know if you can return *haute couture*, Trudy."

Trudy stopped halfway up the stairs, turned around and sank to a step. She buried her face in her hands.

Ben watched her, afraid she might burst into tears. He couldn't stand it when women cried. He tended to do anything, say anything, promise anything, to get them to stop.

Tru snapped her head upright and, from ten feet below her, Ben saw the fire raging in her eyes.

"I was *good* to that woman." Trudy stood, her fists clenched at her side, her teeth gritting as she breathed heavily.

Ben heaved a sigh of relief. Anger was good. Anger he could handle.

She jabbed her finger at the chandelier like it was a human who could hear her. "I did not approve an eighty-five thousand dollar chandelier! You're coming down. If you're not worth anything, you're going to be scrap medal."

Ben stared at her. It wasn't exactly 'as God is my witness, I'll never be hungry again' but it wasn't bad.

"She shouldn't be talking to lamp shades," Eleanor said.

Ben nodded.

Tru charged down the stairs. "Get her on the phone."

Ben took a step back from the guttural voice, afraid Tru's head was going to spin around.

Eleanor stood at the bottom of the stairs, wringing her hands. "Now, Trudy, I don't know if that's best."

Ben rested his fingers on Eleanor's arm to interrupt her. "Tru, look at me." Ben had been a cop for a long time. He knew the tone of voice that got instant results. He didn't yell. He didn't raise his voice or put one ounce of anger in it. But he got her attention.

Tru looked at him, her eyes blazing so fierce Ben had the feeling she was mad at everybody who'd ever pushed her around in her whole, spineless life.

He tried to remember everything she'd taught him. "I don't blame you for being angry."

She bared her teeth at him. He stepped right in front of her. She wouldn't really bite him, would she?

"Trudy Jennings, I'm so proud of you."

Her jaw dropped open. "P...proud?"

"Yes, you've worked so hard and earned so much money and cared for people the whole time you were doing it. You've never said one thing and done another. And I want you to know that it's okay for you to be angry."

"It...it is?" She closed her mouth before any of the flies that buzzed around the chandelier dropped in. "Why is it?"

"Jesus got angry, Tru. When he was faced with a hypocrite or someone who hurt innocent people or who lied and cheated, it made him very angry. It's not a sin to be angry."

Her eyes narrowed. "I don't need your permission to get mad."

"I know you don't." He kept thinking, *soft answer, soft answer*. Great, now *he* was doing a mantra. "That's what I'm trying to say. Because I think, later, when you calm down, you're going to be ashamed of yourself for losing your temper, especially if you phone Liz and yell at her. And I don't want you to do that."

"Yell at her?" Some of the darkest purple eased out of her face.

"No, be ashamed." Ben reached out and rested both hands on Tru's shoulders. He squared her off in front of him. He'd been using his soft answer voice to ease her out of her bad mood. But as he felt his own temper calm and her shoulders relaxing, he knew, for the first time, just how wise Tru's advice was.

"I don't want you to do anything tonight, in the heat of the moment, that you'll regret later."

"But she can't get away with this." There was still heat in Tru's voice, but it was subsiding. When she closed her eyes, the color of her cheeks faded until Ben didn't think he could toast marshmallows on them anymore.

Her head dropped forward. "She's ruined me, Ben. In six months, she's wrecked everything."

"She hasn't wrecked anything important." Ben lifted her chin and her eyes fluttered open. "She hasn't made you less brilliant. She hasn't hurt your soul. She hasn't done anyone bodily harm. All she's done is spent money."

"Money I don't have."

"Money you can make more of." Ben pulled her closer, wishing he could protect her. He'd wanted to toughen her up, but now, when she'd taken a blow hard enough to make a well-done beef steak tougher, he wished he could have spared her.

She let herself rest against him. Trembling with shock and anger, she fit perfectly against him. He rubbed her back and she moved closer.

It struck Ben that there was something else Tru could do in the heat of the moment she might regret later. Or she might *not* regret it. And neither would he.

Eleanor eased herself out of the room.

Ben saw her go out of the corner of his eye, but he never took his attention from Tru. He wasn't about to take advantage of her when she was this upset. He'd done this hero complex thing with sweet-hearted Cara, too. But he couldn't always be the strength for someone else. There came a time when people needed to be strong. He couldn't forget that. He couldn't let this sweet vulnerability trick him into falling for a softie. Not again.

Taking a deep breath, he relaxed his grip.

"Ben, why would she do something like that to me? She wasn't even stealing for herself. She was being flagrant with my money in ways she knew would hurt me. She betrayed my trust." Tru's eyes flashed again.

Ben leaned down until his nose almost touched hers. He spoke, one word at a time. "Turn. The. Other. Cheek."

Silence stretched between them.

He saw the battle inside of her. Her face, so pure and innocent, showed every thought. Ben watched as good and evil warred inside the kindest woman he'd ever met.

At last, with a stricken look, Tru said, "I can make myself say the words, but I don't know if I can ever mean them."

"I don't fault you for honesty. Losing this much money is devastating."

"It's not the money so much as the contempt. She had to know my financial situation. She had to know, especially after the huge down payment on the house, that there was a limit to what I could spend. She deliberately did this to hurt me, while I was paying her the best salary she'd ever had, and giving her more respect than any employer who'd ever hired her."

"How do you know that?"

"She told me. She..." Tru faltered.

"She gossiped about her other employers?"

Tru nodded.

"Do you suppose she was telling the truth?"

Tru's shoulders slumped. "Probably not. Why would she have said a decent word about them when she never had a good word for anyone else? And now she'll go on to another job and say awful things about me to her new boss."

Tru buried her face in her hands. "She could ruin me if she sells an unsavory story about me to the tabloids or some celebrity peep show on television."

Ben smiled since she wasn't watching anyway. She was so sweet.

It'd be hard to ruin her. "My advice is to spend the next few weeks hating her guts then, when you've wallowed enough, get over it and forgive the battle axe."

"So I can call her and scream? Do you think Jesus would consider that turning the other cheek?"

"No, but Jesus has a lot more patience than most people. And he did hate injustice and Liz was unjust to you. No, keep it to yourself. If you do tell her off, she's the kind of woman who might make something out of it. Maybe even record the call and sell it to the highest bidder. You're big enough news and Tru Interventions Jennings bawling out a former employee could generate a lot of bad press."

Ben regretted advising Tru to let Liz go. He'd like to mete out a little frontier justice on Tru's behalf. His mom, the hanging judge, would agree.

She heaved a deep sigh. "Okay, you're right." She looked up the stairs. "What I need is some advice. I need a new personal manager I can trust. I need to find a way to unload all that stuff somehow."

Ben lifted his hands up toward the ceiling. "It's gonna be dark in here."

Tru rubbed her hand over her face then looked up. Shaking her head back and forth, she said, "It really is a pretty lamp shade."

"Not *that* pretty."

She looked at him and at the same second, they began to laugh.

"Tomorrow's Saturday," Ben said. "How about I come over and help you get this whole mess sorted out."

Tru's laughter died but there was still a gleam in her eye and a smile on her face. "I'd like that."

*Whadda ya know? It really works. A soft answer really does turn away wrath.*

# CHAPTER SEVENTEEN

"IT REALLY WORKS, DOESN'T IT, Ben? A soft answer really does turn away wrath. Admit it."

"Is this an 'I told you so'?" Ben laid boxes of Jimmy Choos in the backseat of Tru's Seville.

Trudy watched him like a hawk as they worked inside her garage. "Handle them gently. I don't want so much as a scratch even on the boxes when I return them to the store."

Tru, putting her insomnia to good use, had spent a couple of hours in the middle of the night, researching the return policy of the stores who had dealt with Liz.

"So big deal designers are good about returns, huh?"

"They're great. Eleanor was all wrong about haute couture."

Ben shrugged. "Well, it figures she would be. How would she know anything about hot coats?"

"Hot coats?"

"Yeah, by the way, where are the coats? I haven't seen any of these hot coats you say you're returning."

"Hot coats?" Trudy studied him, trying to read his mind since his mouth wasn't making any sense. "Oh, you mean haute couture?"

"Coats, coaters, whatever."

Trudy decided to forget the explanation. "I sure don't know anything about them, except for what I learned on-line."

"How much sleep did you get?"

"The usual, not much." Trudy rested her boxes beside Ben's. She wasn't used to anyone worrying about her, except Eleanor of course. And she paid Eleanor to worry. Having Ben try and nag her into sleeping better was kind of pleasant. Futile, but pleasant.

"I think the stores are being especially nice to me because I'm about the best customer they've ever had."

"Not after today."

"I'll still have spent a fortune with them. As long as things still have the tags on, they'll take returns, plus, if you just aren't happy they'll take stuff back no questions asked."

"So why aren't you returning everything?"

"Because that's dishonest." Trudy shook her head. "I shouldn't have to explain this to a policeman. Yes, they all cost too much, and I can't afford them, but I've worn them. They're used. The stores can't resell them, and I'm not unhappy with them—except for the price of course. I'm not going to lie."

Ben stopped loading the car and looked at the ceiling of the garage. "I've found a good person, Lord. You don't have to rain fire down on Sodom and Gomorrah."

Trudy giggled. "And after all these go back and the chandelier comes down..."

"The interior design store is okay with that?" Ben tagged along behind her back into the house where Eleanor stacked things. Trudy couldn't help but marvel at having such hard working, attractive help at her disposal.

"Yep, they're even sending an electrician to re-hang the old one...which I found in a third floor bedroom late last night."

"On the weekend?" Ben started gathering boxes.

"Yes. Can you believe it? No charge. They sold me the Chihuly vases, too and they're all going back. They said all these are art pieces and they're all originals. They'll sell right away for more than I paid, so they don't care at all. It's art so it appreciates with age. The jewelry store is taking a bunch of jewelry I've never worn, too."

Trudy carefully bagged a small stack of jewelry boxes. She wished she could dig up her sod and un-sift the beach. "Now, quit changing the subject and admit that I was right about a soft answer turning away wrath."

"It *is* an 'I told you so'? I knew it. That's beneath you." Ben balanced an armload of boxes marked Versace, Dior, Prada and other names Tru had been too foolish to pay attention to.

"You know, you saved me last night."

Ben grinned at her. "Well, you weren't exactly standing on a window ledge, you know. You were just mad."

Trudy stopped and turned around. Ben almost ran into her. "Thank you. This *isn't* an 'I told you so'. This is a thank you."

"I'm being nicer at the precinct, too."

A smile bloomed on Trudy's face. "How's that working out?"

"Okay. Some of the guys are really giving me a hard time about it. Wanna know if I've got six months to live, did I win the lottery, did the doctor put me on Xanax, stuff like that. I may have to pound them to get them to stop. But I promise I'll speak softly the whole time I'm doing it."

Trudy couldn't remember when she'd had so much fun with anybody. "It seems like I spend my whole life controlling my temper. Did you know that?"

"Get moving. Talk while you work."

Trudy turned around.

From behind her, Ben said, "And you don't work too hard controlling your temper around me. You yell at me all the time."

Trudy jogged down the two shallow garage steps and, as she approached the open trunk, she settled the packages in the car and Ben tucked his in beside hers. Standing just inches apart, she wrinkled her nose. "Oh, I'm pretty nice to you sometimes."

Ben's eyes changed. She wouldn't have noticed it if she hadn't been watching him so closely.

Trudy froze and then she burned. Ben leaned down just as she reached up. The kiss felt so nice it scared her to death.

Trudy jumped back just as Ben slipped his arms around her waist. He let go.

Shaking her head, Trudy turned aside and studied the trunk but she didn't see anything, she felt instead. Ben's warmth and strength. Another place for her to hide.

"Ben, I'm sorry but..."

"No, that shouldn't have happened. There's no future in it and I shouldn't have done it."

Trudy frowned and turned to him. "I'm the one who did it and I apologize."

Ben's eyebrows scrunched together. After glaring at her for a full minute he said, "Well, as long as we understand each other. I'm here to protect you, not get involved. It's against regulations, plus you're my teacher. You could be fired for something like this."

Trudy's temper snapped. "It's not exactly like I'm a fifty- year-old professor and you're some innocent eighteen-year-old willing to do anything to get an A, you know."

"So, then it's okay at Bella Vista Christian College for a teacher to get involved with a student?"

"Of course it's not. And we're not involved. I just...we had a moment of..." Trudy wanted to scream and she wasn't sure why. She turned to the house and Ben caught her arm.

Pulled back around, she said, "What?"

"Say it."

Trudy clenched her lips together.

Ben leaned closer. "We had a moment of what, Tru-Blu? Madness? Attraction? What would you call it?"

"I'd call it nothing. I'm planning to forget it."

Ben leaned down and for a moment she wondered if he was going to kiss her again. And she wondered if she was going to let him.

When his nose almost touched hers, he said, "You're a liar."

Trudy backed up a step, in shock.

Ben reeled her back in. "A liar and a coward."

"I am not."

"Call it a mistake if you want."

Trudy's ears started burning. Her cheeks felt hot.

"But don't call it nothing."

"I...I'm not a liar."

"You lie all the time, Tru-Blu. You lie when you give that soft answer back to people you want to belt. You lie when Eleanor and I decide your fate and you stand there and take it. I thought maybe you were coming around when you finally blew your stack last night, but now here you are lying again."

"It's not lying to be polite."

"It is if you tell polite lies."

Trudy wanted to deny it. She wanted to run. "I'm trying to live by a philosophy I believe in. Responding to evil with good doesn't make you a liar. Trying to settle a fight without resorting to violence doesn't make you a coward."

"It's made *you* one."

"B...but you didn't want that kiss any more than I did."

"Oh, I wanted it. But I knew better than to take it. That makes it a mistake."

"Why did you know better?"

Ben looked down, his anger eased from his expression. "Because I've got a hero complex. Because I think I'm some white knight riding to your rescue. You bring out the worst in me."

"This is your worst?" She swallowed hard, charmed. "It seems really great."

"It may be great for a cop. Maybe even for a friend. But trust me, you'd get sick of it if we followed where that kiss wanted to lead."

"I would?" From Ben's grim tone, she knew someone else had gotten sick of Ben's hero complex and had left him scarred.

"It was a mistake." Ben cradled her face. "But it wasn't *nothing*, I won't go that far." He kissed her cheek. "Okay?"

"I'm not right for you, huh?"

"Nope." He sounded so sure, so confident. So sad.

"Well, you're not right for me either, and for the same reason. You'd shelter me from the world, and I've spent too many years hiding. I've failed with the choices I've made in life. I need to help people instead of referring them to someone else. Kissing a white knight is exactly the wrong way to do that."

"You haven't failed."

"I have. And being with you would make it easy for me to go on failing."

Ben shook his head. "We're not going to agree about that, but we agree about the kiss, right?"

Trudy nodded, her throat too tight to answer.

"Good, let's quit making mistakes and get back to work."

# CHAPTER EIGHTEEN

T HEY FINISHED LOADING THE CAR in silence, then backed
the car out of the garage, Ben driving. The car was going back
to the dealer tomorrow. He passed through the gate and, just when
he began to pull out, jammed on the brake so hard Trudy's seatbelt
locked as she jerked against it.

She looked up and followed his gaze to a dark blue luxury car in
a church lot right across the street.

"Watson." Ben's hands strangled the steering wheel.

Watson sat parked in the middle of an empty lot. Trudy knew
the restraining order called for him to not get within 500 feet of
her. She'd bet he'd measured the distance out to the inch.

Trudy reached across the seat to clutch Ben's arm, so grateful for
his presence. "Was he there last night?"

Ben stared, his eyes narrow. Trudy could almost see his cop's
brain sorting details. "No."

The windows of the Mercedes were tinted, but Watson's hulking
shape lurked behind the wheel.

"If we approach him, the restraining order doesn't require that
he back off. He's legal sitting there."

"All the time?" Trudy thought of her wrought iron gate. "He
can see all the way to the house. He might be able to see in some
of the windows if he's got binoculars."

Ben added with quiet menace, "Or a telephoto lens."

Trudy shuddered. "You think he'd take pictures of us?"

Ben looked away from Watson for the first time. "Us? No, not
us. He'd take pictures of *you* though. You said your bedroom has is
on the lake front, right?"

Trudy's lungs quit working. She could feel Watson's eyes burning her flesh.

"If he comes on your beach he violates the restraining order. We could convince the judge he's stalking you and make the charges stick."

Trudy thought of the man on her beach that night. She'd never seen him since. But if it hadn't been for the lightning, she wouldn't have seen him then. Watson could be coming onto her property every night.

"I'm going to call Eleanor and warn her he's out here," Trudy said through clenched teeth. "Let's get out of here. I may cash in that chandelier for a Doberman."

"You can get two hundred Dobermans for that price of that chandelier." Ben pulled into an opening in the traffic. "Then you'd *really* need your sand sifted."

Trudy's nerves were wound to the breaking point by the time the electrician left with the ridiculous chandelier.

Watson skulked outside and her finances blew up inside. That lacey iron security gate was a pathetic barrier between her and Watson's clawing hands.

Trudy nearly staggered when she went into her living room, shaken from what the electrician had said. "I didn't get any cash for the chandelier. Liz charged so many other things, returning it only cleared the debt."

"I'm sorry, Tru." Ben followed her into the room. "At least you returned enough to settle the charge accounts in all the stores and closed the accounts in case Liz gets any weird ideas about using them."

She sank onto her over-stuffed, over-priced leather couch. "Yes, and I'm glad of that. But I'm going to be in trouble trying to pay my mortgage.

"How much is it? Maybe I could help you out until things settle down."

"Eleven thousand dollars." Trudy pulled out of her self-pity when Ben collapsed on the couch.

"Eleven thousand dollars a month?"

Trudy nodded, watching Ben try to close his mouth.

"Can you refinance? Can you sell?"

She was grateful he didn't ask if she could grow a brain. "I can't refinance. I've only lived here a few months."

"Six, I suppose. You bought it right after you hired Liz on her advice, right?"

Trudy nodded. "It would sell for a good price, this property goes up steadily, but I doubt I'd make a profit with all the bank charges and real estate fees. I'd be lucky to break even. It was a ridiculous purchase but Liz convinced me it'd be a great tax deduction."

"You'd get out from under an eleven thousand dollar a month payment though."

"And I'd move in somewhere that would be even more vulnerable to Watson." She looked over her shoulder. The large picture window had heavy, no doubt expensive drapes, pulled closed. She half expected to see Watson standing behind her.

"But that's what I'm going to have to do. I've got quarterly taxes due this month, too. Don't even think about what the utility bill is on this place." Trudy nodded. "I'll list it tomorrow. I've got to. Even if more money comes in quick, I'll need every penny of it for taxes."

Trudy dropped her face into her hands. "If I can't pay them it'll be on all the news shows. Just like when Willy Nelson got in trouble for not paying taxes."

"You're assuming Liz paid your taxes while she's been here."

Trudy's head snapped up, her eyes got as round as an owl's.

Ben surged to his feet. "Where do you keep your tax forms?"

They raced into Liz's office.

"What if she hasn't been paying them?" Trudy started digging through the desk.

It was the day that wouldn't end. By the time they'd gone through everything Trudy realized, even if the house sold quickly, she was going to be in deep financial water for a very long time."

"Call your lawyer on Monday. Get them to work on making this right with the government." Ben rubbed her back and the gentle support he offered was the only thing holding her together.

"Accept every booking on every show that makes you an offer. Think of it as being 'On the Road Again' just like Willie. Get your next book polished up and sent off to the publisher. Royalty checks come in regularly. If the house sells quickly, any profit you make can go toward back taxes and the interest and penalties."

"Surely there's a crime involved in the way she mismanaged my money."

"There are several," Ben said. "And if we can prove she ran you into the red maliciously, we can turn it into some jail time. But the bottom line is, she didn't take any of it for herself. She was earning a very hefty salary, but you agreed to that and Tru, you're responsible for the money you spent. You, not your personal manager."

"I know." Trudy closed her eyes. "I deserve this. I spend my life spouting stupid theories about how other people should fix their lives. I'm a fool who has no right to...to..." Trudy's voice broke and with it, her control. She began to sob.

Ben pulled her into his strong arms.

She cried for a long time, underneath the humiliation and the betrayal of her trust, was fear. Fear of public ridicule, fear of bill collectors and IRS auditors, fear of Watson.

After the worst of the storm of tears, Ben said, "You don't spout stupid theories. You speak the truth."

Ben pulled away from her and tilted her chin up. "And Tru-Blu, the only way you fail in any of this is if, now that things are tough, you turn your back on your beliefs. Now is the time that God is really calling you to stand up and deliver all that love and strength you write about so beautifully."

Trudy hiccupped as she listened to this cynical man give her the soft answers that were the basis of her faith. "God's love for me. My love for Him."

"Your love for others."

Ben pulled a neatly folded handkerchief out of his pocket and wiped the tears from her face with gentle patience. His touch was more than care, it was a caress.

She looked in his eyes and remembered what he'd said.

Her love for others.

For the first time she thought about that love in terms of Ben. With his heroic nature, he saw her as fragile and needy. As their eyes locked and the way he held her became a hug, she thought of him that first night. When he'd saved her from Watson. He'd become her knight-in-shining armor. Standing there, her gaze locked with his she couldn't trust herself because right now, trapped by circumstances with him, this felt enough like love to confuse her.

For a moment Ben bend closer. His arms tightened. He might be just as confused as she was. Then his head turned away as if he was physically forcing his eyes to look elsewhere.

Ben gave his head a shake that was tiny, at the same time it was fierce.

"I'd better get out of here."

Ben rested the handkerchief in her hand and stepped away. "Here keep this. If all else fails, you can move into my place, and I'll bunk with Scott until things straightened out."

He took another step back. Trudy took a step forward.

He held up his hands as if to ward her off. "I've got to go now or something might happen we'd both regret."

It was the hardest thing she'd ever done, but she forced herself to nod.

Ben turned and charged out of the room. She heard him shout, "Eleanor. I'm leaving. Double check the security system after I go."

The front door slammed and his truck roared to life. He drove away.

Leaving her alone.

Not alone, Watson hovered nearby.

Her insomnia had never been worse.

The lights extinguished, she compulsively checked on Watson's car. She hated that he was there. Then, around two, he was gone. That was even worse. Was he creeping closer to her house? Was he on her beach?

Trudy went back to her room through the darkened upstairs. Every whistle of the wind was a human moan. Every pulse of the waves sounded like the heavy breathing of a madman.

She tried to write the last chapter of her book. It was always a triumph of the Lord. His scripture, His victory, His love shining out of Trudy's little self-help books. She knew her success had come from the Lord. And now she couldn't hear His voice. That was her own failure, not God's.

Watson's presence was a living thing outside her bedroom window. Whether he sat out there or not, it chiseled into her peace of mind. She flipped on the tiny reading lamp, feeling as if she was exposing herself to him, though the window was off to the side.

Lifting her well worn Bible and resting it against her chest, she read the Proverb God had given her as a life verse.

*A soft answer turns away wrath, but a harsh word stirs up anger.*

The Bible fell open a second later to Jesus during His precious Sermon on the Mount, saying *"If someone strikes you on one cheek, turn to him the other, also."*

The whole section of Luke dealt with loving enemies. How had Watson become her enemy? What had she ever done to make that happen? Trudy cried out to God, to find love for Watson and Liz. Even if Trudy could force herself to love, forgiveness was another matter. She couldn't find it in her heart, but God didn't give her a choice.

Hugging her Bible to her, she wrestled with hate, as surely as Jacob had spent a long night wrestling with an angel. Only this time, it was God Who held on and Trudy who wanted to get away.

"How can I forgive a man who would hurt me if he had the chance? How can I forgive a woman who would spit on me when I said 'I forgive you?' Don't they have to want forgiveness?"

*Did the centurions want forgiveness from My Son as He hung on that cross dying?*

One did, Trudy remembered.

*But my Son forgave them all.*

"Father, forgive them." Trudy said the words and hoped her heart would follow.

When it didn't, she knew what she really needed to say. "Father, forgive me."

Wrecked with exhaustion, she fell asleep as dawn began to light the sky, still as angry as she'd been when she crawled into bed. With no forgiveness in her heart, Trudy failed in her first real spiritual test. She couldn't, wouldn't find it in her heart to turn the other cheek.

# CHAPTER NINETEEN

BEN PICKED TRU AND ELEANOR up the next morning and went to church with them. After the service, Ben felt helpless as Trudy kept an appointment with the woman who had sold her the pink mansion and put it back on the market.

When they approached Tru's driveway, Ben saw Watson standing against his car in his usual parking lot spot, his legs crossed as he leaned back and stretched into a friendly wave when Tru's car passed by.

Ben gritted his teeth and muttered "Jerk" as they drove past. Instead of going inside Tru's house, he walked to his truck and followed her to the car dealership to return the Seville.

When they headed back, Watson sat in his car, his arm stretched across the back of the seat. Ben glared at him just as Watson turned his head and lifted his hand in a friendly gesture.

After pacing for an hour, Tru flicked the curtains open an inch and announced, "He's gone."

Ben watched Eleanor rest her hands on Tru's shoulders.

"Get away from the window, honey." Eleanor guided Tru away, but when Eleanor left the room, Tru returned to the window and glanced outside again.

With bills spread out in front of him, Ben tried to make sense of Tru's finances. Her pacing and window peeking was getting on his nerves. He knew she had a clear view of Watson's parking spot— just as Watson had a clear shot of her home.

Earlier, Ben had sent police officers to run him off but Watson hadn't budged. The two officers walked inside with stone faces.

Herb Wilson, a sergeant Ben had known for years, rested a hand on his gun. "Says the view inspires his writing. Even showed us some of his work, on his laptop."

The other uniform, a rookie, jerked a shoulder at Ben. "He lawyered up, on the phone. Said he had every right to a public parking lot, that he wasn't breaking any laws."

When the officers left, Ben watched Tru pace with her arms crossed, glancing at the draped window every few seconds.

*Where was her peace? Where was that kind heart and those soft answers?* Ben hurt for.

It was the first time God had asked Trudy to give, and she'd abandoned Him. She was a failure. A failure. *A failure.*

Ben passed his midterms with flying colors and he hadn't snorted in class for a month. When he occasionally couldn't act as her chauffeur, he sent a policeman in a squad car to escort her. She always went all out for Halloween because they had so many trick-or-treaters come to the neighborhood. This year she left her lights off, afraid to leave her gate open.

And the letters came and the emails and phone calls and Watson sat in that parking lot and watched her until she wanted to scream.

And Ben very politely didn't kiss her again.

The big jerk.

And then Trudy found out Eleanor wasn't going to her daughter's house for Thanksgiving.

"You haven't missed Thanksgiving with Jenny in years, Eleanor. You can't stay here with me and neglect your family." Trudy's stomach wrenched when she thought of being here alone for five days. Eleanor's daughter lived in Denver and Eleanor and her four children made a huge effort to spend this holiday together every year. Eleanor had told Trudy that many times.

"You don't dare be in this house by yourself." Eleanor paused, and looked thoughtful, "Unless you want to come? Get away from here for a few days. It'd be good for you."

Trudy didn't have a functioning credit card anymore. She'd closed every account. Something she regretted now, but when she'd sworn to get her debts settled it had seemed brilliant. She didn't even have a bank debit card, and if she had…she still didn't have the money for a ticket.

"Let me buy you a ticket to Denver, honey," Eleanor said, even though Trudy hadn't said a word about the cost of the ticket.

"No, absolutely not. Your daughter doesn't have room for all of you. And I'd throw a wet blanket over your holiday fun with all my troubles." Trudy would have liked to get away, but she knew Eleanor needed a break as much as she did and taking Trudy along would disrupt the family get together.

"I'm staying home. I wouldn't rest easy for one minute knowing you're here alone."

Ben came in on the tail end of their negotiations.

"If you won't go with Eleanor, then come out to the ranch with me. My folks always have people in and out. The house is huge, we rattle around even when all six of us are there. You can stay the whole time Eleanor is gone."

Trudy turned to look at Ben. "Six kids in the family?"

He'd talked about his twin brother Brett some. Ben mentioned he was better looking than his brother, taller, smarter and nicer.

Trudy laughed.

"I don't get together much with Brett anymore. We were both in the service then we worked in the war zone with a private security firm for a while. The life just didn't suit him."

"You're not close with your twin brother anymore?"

Ben shook his head. "I don't think about it much. We're both busy and live such different lives. And Brett's got a veterinary clinic way out in the country. He doesn't come to town much."

"That's sad."

Ben shrugged. "It is a little now that I think about it."

"Will the rest of your family be there?" He'd mentioned having a big family on other occasion but there'd been few details.

"Most won't. Deb is the oldest…and by the way she loves it when I say that."

Trudy smiled.

"She can't get away from the governor's office for more than a day. Next year is an election year and she's a co-manager of his campaign. She's probably going to be riding on a Thanksgiving Day float somewhere. Jim is second and he's with Parks and Wildlife. He's a game warden who can usually get to holiday gatherings.

"Next is Case. He works for the Justice Department out of DC. We're not sure doing what. We haven't heard a word from him in a year and a half, but he's gone undercover before. It's weird but we're used to it. We'll see him when we see him. My little sister Beth is planning to come over on Saturday and Sunday. She's a detective for the Houston PD. She's a hostage negotiator and she always has to take her turn on-call, but she got the weekend off. And we're used to her not making it if trouble breaks. Jimbo is almost for sure coming but Mom's panicking that it might be only me and Brett for dinner."

Ben leaned close and whispered, "She thinks we're trouble makers, can you believe it?"

Trudy smiled. Lately she only smiled when Ben was around. The rest of the time she felt like she was surrounded by the malevolent spirit of Ralph Watson.

Even now, able to smile, she felt like the whole world, outside the walls of her house, roiled with hatred. With a madman waiting for a chance to grab her.

Or maybe holding back on that because he still clung to the sheerest thread of sanity.

One day he'd snap. Or she'd make a mistake that put herself in his hands. Or both. And he'd come. Until that day, she felt him watching and waiting and coming.

"No, thank you, but I'll be fine here." She would be absolutely wretched. "Was Watson out there?" Going to his house was out of the question. She didn't want to inflict herself on his family.

"Come with me," Eleanor insisted.

"No, she's coming to my parents' house," Ben came up to pat Trudy on the arm.

Being taken care of could feel a lot like being pushed around sometimes. Trudy found her inner 'Liz' and said, "Absolutely not. You're both going and I'm staying and that's final."

He picked her up on his way out of town.

He'd grumbled about hauling all her suitcases and told her to leave her laptop behind so she could get away from work, but in the end, he'd loaded everything. Now that they were rolling, he was cheerful again. "This thing is great to handle."

"Are you sure you wouldn't like to drive?" Ben grinned across his console at her.

"I'd take out swaths of cars."

"It's Texas. There's plenty of space. I'll let you behind the wheel once we're out of town."

Trudy wondered how she'd ended up in this pick-up, with this man, on the way to a stranger's house for a holiday. If she could've afforded it, she'd've flown to Florida to see her aunt. A woman who lived in a one-bedroom apartment in an assisted living center. It was a nice place. And Trudy hadn't seen her for a while. And Auntie's couch couldn't be as short as she remembered.

The drive was an hour… Trudy didn't want to judge the distance because Ben was taking advantage of Texas' generous speed limit and maybe pushing it beyond. She'd trained herself to not look at the speedometer.

Ben seemed determined to entertain her. They didn't talk about Watson, or class work, although he tended to try and wheedle an 'A' out of her often enough, she'd learned it was his idea of a joke.

Then, out in the middle of nowhere, on a nice four-lane highway that seemed odd considering they only met a car every ten miles or so, Ben slowed and turned off the highway, and drove under a huge arched sign over a gravel drive-way. The massive wood sign had 'Garrison' carved into the wood and painted black. It looked like it had been branded into the dark oak. Perched atop the peak of the arch, the oak formed a circle, branded into it were the letters G and R intertwined.

Garrison Ranch.

As they drove under the arch, Trudy said, "I've been feeling like the worst kind of intruder, Ben, but thank you. Driving away from my house, leaving town, being alone on the road so I'm sure we weren't followed." She closed her eyes and inhaled deeply. "It's a good feeling. It's like the pressure is lifting off my neck."

"We haven't talked about it, Trudy, but you're going to be moving once the house is gone. Why don't you come out here during the Christmas break?"

"You think this will still be going on at Christmas time?" Trudy had to admit she'd given up on it ever ending.

"We'll see what Watson does when he can't find you. Maybe he'll make a mistake and we can nail him."

"I can't do that." Trudy remembered vividly refusing to come to Thanksgiving with him, yet here she was. She'd have to be really tough. "That reminds me, I need to make a big show out of moving. I don't want Watson to hurt the people who move in. If he knows I'm gone, he'll leave them alone."

Trudy hoped new owners would show interest in a lot of Trudy's furniture—the pieces she hadn't been able to return. She wanted an apartment so she wouldn't need much and she was dreading the work of a big move.

They drove for miles through winding roads, broad expanses of waving grass on both sides of them, until a ranch house came into sight.

It wasn't massive. Trudy had been afraid that the sign was an indicator. But it was nice. Rustic and old and beautiful with what looked like a couple of additions on an older home, but all in nice harmony.

"How long has your family lived here?"

"This house was built originally by my great-grandfather when he first went out on his own. It was about a fourth the size, and Great-Grandpa used to say he'd thought he'd built it plenty big."

"You knew him? You were born while your great-grandfather was still alive?"

"Yep, I remember when he died. I was ten years old. Great old man, tough and cranky when his arthritis acted up, but he had a great heart and loved to tell me stories of the old days. My grandpa built his own place and great-grandma and grandpa moved in with him in their later years and opened this house up. Dad and mom had been living in town, a forty-mile drive away, but Mom was a lawyer at first so Dad said he'd rather commute than her. But when great-grandpa moved out they had four kids and were bursting at the seams in their house in town. They moved in. Mom cut back her hours for a few years while the babies were coming. Then when she got a judicial nomination that took her to Dallas, she bought an airplane, learned to fly and starting commuting."

"You talk about them with a lot of affection. They must be great people."

"They are great people. Uh, there may be a little tension between me and Brett. Well, everyone and Brett. We all love each other, but he's happiest out working with his animals and he doesn't stay in touch very well. We're not close like you'd think twins would be."

Ben drove right around the house. Back here she saw a corral with several horses, a huge old red barn and a newer metal machine shed. And a second shed, low and sleek, with an oversized garage door open to show a small plane.

There was a five-car garage and, as they pulled up, a short haired dog came running toward them barking.

Back here the Garrison's prosperity was much more noticeable. Ben stopped right beside a beige Camry.

Ben popped his door open.

"Did you tell them what was going on with me?" Trudy asked.

"I did, just a little." Then he gave a rueful smile. "I should have asked you first, but telling them was the only way I could convince them I wasn't bringing a girlfriend home. I tried 'lonely friend with nowhere to go for the holidays' and they just weren't buying it."

"It's okay. If you'd've discussed telling them, I would've said no, then you'd have nagged me until I said yes, probably. That's how you got me into your truck."

His grin turned to high beam. "That is how it worked, Tru-Blu. Come on in and meet my family."

The back door opened and a man stepped out who had to be Brett, the twin brother. If she'd gotten the report right, the oldest brother Jim would be here but he had a full beard and dressed like a lumber jack. This man wasn't Jim.

Brett didn't look much like Ben. He was a bit shorter, his hair a light brown, well cut, as opposed to Ben's dark curls that he tended to neglect. But Brett had the same blue eyes and flashing smile.

He gave Ben a quiet smile.

She could just bet their mama thought they were troublemakers.

The air was crisp and cool. She heard cattle mooing in the distance. Brett's eyes shifted from his brother to Trudy. His smile was bigger, more relaxed. Trudy noticed he didn't greet Ben with a hug or even a handshake.

Instead he came to her door, swung it open, those same gentleman-ly manners Ben had, and said, "Hi, I'm Brett, the good-looking twin. Come on in."

Trudy hopped out, swung open the back door and pulled out her plastic pie carrier. "I brought a pumpkin pie."

Brett froze. His eyes went wide as he looked at the carrier. "You made it yourself?"

Smiling, she said, "Yep, even the crust. My grandma taught me how to make a pie and do it right."

"Will you marry me?" Brett slung his arm around her and dragged her toward the house.

She looked over her shoulder at Ben, who grinned and shrugged one shoulder. She realized she'd hope for some flash of jealousy and was ashamed of herself.

"No, but I appreciate the offer. You're a veterinarian, right?"

"Yep, while my little brother here was being all show-off with the special forces, I got to work with parade horses and such. The military got me through Vet school. So, I'm a Vet who's a Vet." He smirked like he'd told that joke a thousand times."

"He had to do some tough stuff," Ben said. "He was decent at hand-to-hand combat and a good shot. But he'd rather pet the horses."

"Sounds like a smart guy to me." Trudy tried to be subtle when she stepped sideways so he wasn't holding her.

They reached the house and the aroma of turkey almost brought tears to Trudy's eyes. It had been years since she'd been to a real family Thanksgiving. When she'd gone to live with Grandma and Auntie after the wreck that killed her parents, they'd done their best to fill the gaps left. And they were great, loving women. But the heavy lifting fell more to Trudy from an early age. She could make a good turkey and a great pie but her gravy was only borderline. Although Grandma had never stopped bragging on her.

Mrs. Garrison, the hanging judge, turned from where she stirred something in a huge bowl and smiled. "Welcome to the Garrison Ranch."

The kind smile, the generous greeting, the luscious smells...to Trudy it felt like coming home.

"Mrs. Garrison, everything was delicious." Trudy stood with her hands in dishwater while Janet Garrison did everything else. But Trudy kept busy.

The men had helped to an impressive degree, but they'd finally deserted the field to watch football and Hangin' Judge Janet Garrison and Trudy were alone.

"I've read all of your books, Trudy." Janet stuffed a final covered platter in the huge refrigerator, then straightened and grabbed a dish cloth. "I think they're wonderful. And I've seen you on the morning shows. I feel like I've got a real celebrity in my home. A guru."

Trudy rinsed off the last pot and handed it to her hostess. "A guru who tells others how to live their lives and has managed to mess up her own. I'm sure they'll strip my guru badge off of me any minute."

Janet finished with the pot and said, "Let's sit down for a minute. Ben told me some of your troubles, Trudy. I can look into things if you want. Put some pressure on to get the restraining order changed, make the distance he has to stay from you larger so you don't have to see him watching you."

As Trudy settled in at the kitchen table, she said, "Ben thinks when I move that will change how the restraining order works. Once I'm in an apartment I'll probably never be able to see him."

"You're losing your house and you've sold your car?"

"Yep," Trudy liked the kindness in Janet's eyes. And the sharp intelligence. It was a terrific combination. She swallowed hard. "Do you think there's a point to changing the restraining order now?"

"I can look into it if you want. Watson sitting nearby watching you is behavior that I'd consider threatening."

"He claims it's a beautiful view that inspires his writing. He even said he's been there for a long time, I just never noticed him until he started asking for my help."

Janet poured them both a cup of coffee. She was slender and small boned. She'd cast a big shadow in Trudy's mind. No doubt the 'Hangin' Judge' nickname made her seem larger.

"I'll see what I can find. Now, tell me about being Ben's teacher. He said he thought at first he was going to get sent to the principal's office, and his father and I would have to come in to get him out. It wouldn't be the first time."

Trudy smiled, then chuckled. Janet broke into laughter and Trudy felt most of the weight lift off her shoulders. She was glad she'd come.

"I'm so glad I came, Ben. Thank you." They'd stayed four days.

Trudy had been afraid everyday they'd have to go home. Jim, everyone called him Jimbo, had only come for Thanksgiving Day. It seemed that people tended to act up in state parks on holiday weekends.

When Ben's little sister Beth showed up on Saturday midday, the party started all over again and Janet Garrison made a second turkey. They'd just barely worked up another appetite.

And now, as they drove toward home, Trudy thought of Watson for the first time in days.

"I'll get the house sold. I'll rent an apartment with a secure entrance and I'll probably feel safer there than I do at home." That wouldn't be much of a contest. Home felt dangerous. It'd be hard for anywhere else to feel worse.

As they approached Long Pine, her tension slowly returned, like an old clock that wound tighter and tighter. Watson, her money troubles, finding a place to live…when she couldn't afford anything for rent.

The tension coiled but she could handle it. She was rested. She'd taken a step back and had taken the time to pray and let go of all the panic she felt. She could face her troubles with some perspective.

"I don't like having to be so careful where I go, but honestly, he hasn't approached me again. It's creepy him sitting out there watching, but he will have to give up, or he'll finally do something really criminal to someone else, since he can't get to me."

Trudy shook her head. "That sounds awful. Like I want someone to get hurt."

Ben reached over and patted her arm. "I know what you mean. You've done your part, Trudy, by reporting him. I'm sorry we couldn't throw away the key but you're right. He seems to be in some mad little world of his own over there. Watching you house and typing his books.

"Being with your family for Thanksgiving gave me a chance to feel safe and find my balance."

"Did you get some sleep?" He got off the highway and drove down the street that connected to her neighborhood.

No one knew about her insomnia besides Eleanor. It was interesting to have someone want to talk about it.

They pulled through her gate in the late afternoon and the sunset made the pink glow.

They got out. "Eleanor's plane should be landing about now. She should be home in an hour."

"I'll wait around so you're not here alone."

Trudy would have assured him that wasn't necessary if she'd had any hope he'd go. He wouldn't, and she was so glad of that.

They went inside and Trudy stumbled to a halt and screamed.

"What is it?" Ben always went in first. But today they'd been too relaxed. And Trudy had to face the destruction without warning.

Ben said a word that broke a couple of commandments, then he pulled Trudy outside. She screamed and fought his grip, then she stumbled backward and tripped on her stairs and fell to the ground.

Ben wasn't quick enough to catch her. She was on her feet and running before he could help her up.

He caught her and she screamed and flailed her arms. He restrained her and spoke low hard words into her ear. "We're getting back in the truck."

She shuddered deeply, but the screaming cut off. Gasping for breath, sobs breaking from her throat, he held her until the worst of the terror passed.

Then when she finally quit fighting him and clung, he called for backup.

He explained what had happened. "The paint looks dry and he's probably long gone."

Trudy's head came up. Their eyes met and they wheeled around to look at the spot where Watson always sat. He was there. Ben took one long stride toward him then stopped.

He couldn't go thrash the guy. First because it was wrong. Second because it would give Watson plenty to complain to his lawyer about. Third because Trudy was watching.

He swung his truck door open. Trudy scrambled in so fast he didn't have time to help her. Ben rounded the front end and climbed in behind the wheel. He started the truck and turned it so they could keep an eye on Watson.

He was gone.

They'd given him what he wanted. Terror, screaming, tears.

Ben asked for forgiveness for the language and prayed for a lightning strike to fry Ralph Watson.

Eleanor pulled in. Trudy could see her grim expression before she got out of her sturdy little Ford Escape.

Trudy had been sitting alone, numb, for most of the last hour, once her panic had subsided. Ben was inside with the other detectives, but Trudy knew with sick certainty that there wouldn't be a fingerprint anywhere.

Sliding down from the truck, she walked between two patrol cars with their lights flashing and past a pick-up, almost as flashy as Ben's, that two investigators had driven up.

"What happened?" But Eleanor didn't sound afraid, not even very surprised.

Trudy'd been surprised.

"Watson vandalized the house."

Eleanor gasped, then furrows of anger etched the corners of her mouth and furrowed her brow. "Why can't they stop him. This is ridiculous."

"They're searching for some way to prove it's him right now." Her voice was so sharp it could cut. She inhaled slowly, noticed her arms were crossed so tightly her arms were numb. She forced herself to relax. "I only stepped in the door. I haven't seen anything else. Ben said I have to stay out here while the crime scene techs work."

"How did he get in? Why didn't the security alarm go off and alert the police?"

Shaking her head, Trudy said, "I don't know much."

She described what she'd seen.

Eleanor pulled her into her arms. "What if you'd been home."

A shudder wracked Trudy's whole body. She forced herself to remain calm. "He probably only went in because he knew I wasn't there."

"He's a madman, Trudy. They've got to be able to prove he did this and lock him up."

Trudy had serious doubts they'd find what they needed to stop him. And now the question was, could she even stay here? And if not here, then where? She'd be hard pressed to pay her rent once she got out from under her house payments. She sure couldn't afford a place until she retired her mortgage. And who knew what damage was done. Selling the house had just gotten a lot harder.

She discussed what had to be done with Eleanor, glad she'd had time to calm down. It'd taken her close to forty-five minutes to think beyond horror. And now she was working up her backbone to face that house. And live there. Her backbone stiffened and for the first time she got mad. Watson wasn't going to drive her out of her house.

So, Trudy where can I drive you?" Ben finally finished with the crime scene. He'd pushed them hard to go over every surface. Hoping they'd find fingerprints. Hoping they could end this.

It was a rich neighborhood so he didn't have to push real hard. The police were here in force and doing a good job.

Now he had to get Trudy out of here. And she tended to resist him when she should just do as she was told.

He tried to imagine how she'd react if he told her that.

"I'm staying the night with Eleanor."

Ben was so braced for an argument, he almost stumbled forward when she was so agreeable.

"I'll stay with her until the house is cleaned up. I've already phoned the insurance company. Eleanor will meet them here first thing in the morning."

"Ben, you bring her to my place," Eleanor waited until he nodded, then headed for her car. "I'll head on home and get things ready for company."

They watched Eleanor drive away.

"I need to see the house. Is there a lot of damage?"

"It's bad."

Their eyes met. Every instinct he had was to protect her and that included shielding her from what was inside that house.

But meeting her eyes, he was reminded that she was no fool. She had to suspect what was in there and she was going in anyway. Honestly, her imagination might be worse than the truth. Just as well to let her see it.

"You brought a lot of clothes out to my folks' house this weekend."

"I remember you teased me about overpacking, but it was for four days. I didn't know if your family dressed up for Thanksgiving or if we'd go to church together. I thought we might end up hiking or riding horses. The weather sounded warm but this time of year—"

"Yes, I teased you, but now I'm glad you overpacked. We can sort through things in the house and maybe find some stuff, but I'm thinking that what's in those suitcases is about all you own."

Trudy frozen, then turned her head to look at him.

"My clothes?"

He should just take her in and let her see. Did it help to prepare her ahead of time, or was he making things worse? "Let's go in."

He rested one hand on her back as they walked toward the house. "He slashed things, dumped drawers out. Except for that messed up poster of you—which might be his idea of a leaving you a calling card—all the damage is in your room. I'd say you get some painters in there and a bunch of trash bags, you can have it cleared out in a day and the painting done about that fast. But you won't have many clothes left."

Trudy turned back to the house. "I've got to g-go in and look."

Ben put his hand gently on her arm. "Let Eleanor handle this. Let her hire painters and a cleaning service."

"With what money?" Her voice rose with despair.

She'd been calm and happy out at the ranch and even pretty steady on the drive home. The fact that Watson robbed her of that so brutally the minute she came home made Ben want to find the man and serve up a little frontier justice.

"Your insurance company should pay for that and the painters. I remember seeing bills for insurance and you've got a big policy. For once Liz's overspending is working for you. Why don't you just let Eleanor handle all of it. It's ugly. It's the kind of thing that you can't unsee."

Nodding, Trudy said, "Poor Eleanor." She inhaled slowly and let the breath out just as slowly. He saw her lips move and could read them.

"Soft answer, soft answer, soft answer."

Then she snapped her head around. Her eyes blazed with anger. "I'd like to beat Watson to within an inch of his life. I'm not proud of that."

She jerked on the door handle and got out. Without looking back, she marched for the house. Ben scrambled to catch up with her.

The poster was gone.

"Thank you for taking it down." She paused on the threshold. There was a flat wall a few paces in from the front door. Ugly strips of red paint showed on the wall with an almost perfect clean rectangle. An ugly gouge marked the wall where the knife had been embedded. One of her publicity photos, blown up to poster size and painted with garish splashes of red. It had been slashed, then two pairs of scissors pinned it to the wall. One of the scissors through an eye, the other through her throat.

"It was evidence." Ben put his hand on her back and the warmth steadied her.

He tried to sound professional, but he couldn't keep the concern from is voice. She remembered him kissing her. A mistake, he'd said. But he wouldn't pretend to forget it.

She wanted to throw herself in his arms and make another mistake. But she'd be reaching for him out of weakness. And she didn't want that.

"Except for this and the broken window in the back, everything that's wrecked is in your room." His hand pressed a bit closer and she realized they hadn't moved. She was leaning on him. She straightened and headed for the stairs.

"Why didn't my alarm go off? I know I set it."

"We checked. It's not working. I'm afraid you might not have paid the bill."

Trudy stopped dead in her tracks, in the middle of the staircase. She turned to him with narrow eyes. "I know I paid it. I'm sure."

"We'll call tomorrow and find out what happened then."

"A little late to find out now." With a look of frustrated fury, she whirled around and charged up the stairs.

Inside her room she took one glance, then covered her eyes with both hands. Breathing in, holding it together, she forced herself to look.

Her bedding was torn from the bed and slashed to ribbons. The pillows were cut up until the stuffing had exploded all over the room, as if he'd stabbed them in a frenzy.

Her drawers were pulled out and dumped, the drawers cast aside. The closet door was open and she could see the wreckage in there, clothes piled deep on the floor, all hacked to bits.

He'd destroyed things, then scattered them on the floor until the carpet was barely visible. She liked her clothes and heaven knew what she owned was valuable thanks to Liz, but she didn't really care about these things, she only cared about the shocking signs of violence and a hate so vivid it hit her like a closed fist.

"The bathroom is just as bad. Make up bottles smashed. Shampoo, every lotion and oil you own is spilled all over. Insurance will replace it, but that doesn't change how frightening this is."

His hand was still there.

"I lived with my grandma after my parents' death in a car accident. I'd been with her a couple of years when I had my purse stolen at school and I was crying. I remember her hugging me and saying, "Don't cry over anything that can't cry over you."

Trudy turned from the destruction. "It always struck me as really wise. And I could measure almost everything against the pain of losing Mom and Dad. So, I took it to heart. I won't cry, but I'm going to need a lot more prayer to get through my anger."

Ben said, "Maybe prayers and a punching bag. Just to take the edge off."

The shock of humor wrung a smile out of her, when she would've thought a smile was beyond her right now.

"I wouldn't want to break my typing fingers."

"Maybe you can buy some boxing gloves with the insurance money."

That got another smile.

It must've encouraged him to go on being outrageous. "The insurance company is going to be shocked to find out how many designer clothes you have. They'll probably drop you after this is over."

"That's okay. I'm moving out." Her shoulders slumped to think that she was starting over. What a failure she was. "I'll probably drop the insurance company before they can drop me."

# CHAPTER TWENTY

THEY'D FOUND NOTHING TO TIE the vandalism to Watson. Eleanor's apartment was small but nice and completely affordable. It wasn't lost on Trudy that her housekeeper, in her modest apartment, was a lot smarter with her money than Trudy.

On the Friday after Watson's attack, the house was fixed and it was time to go home.

Ben came to pick her up and Trudy hurried out and climbed into his truck before he could shift it into park. She knew Ben would fight her, but she'd win.

"Two things happened today." She'd just get it all out before he could protest and she'd give him the good news first.

Well, not good. But the news that was less likely to set him off.

"I found out the security system was off because someone can-celled it. Liz was their contact, so it was probably her."

"Not Watson?" Ben was immediately alert.

"They said it was done online with a request to cancel and refund any money. The system is password protected. Liz would have that info. I don't think it's written down anywhere for Watson to steal."

"So, the system is back up and running?" Ben started rolling toward the exit of the parking lot.

"Yes, they hadn't gotten around to refunding the payment yet, so they just switched it back on. And I set up a new password. And Eleanor said the painters are done and everything's cleaned up. And she moved me into another bedroom, I have eight."

"I also contacted some stores about returning furniture. I found receipts and a lot of the bedding still had price tags on them.

The mattresses hadn't been unwrapped from their plastic bags. Liz must've paid for them in full because there are no credit card payments showing, but I know where it came from. I saw the delivery truck once."

Ben hit the brakes hard and Trudy jerked against her seatbelt. He turned to her, incredulous. "You saw the delivery truck? That's how you know where it came from? Didn't you pick it out?"

Trudy looked at him and shrugged. "I let Liz handle it."

Ben made that rude noise…the one he no longer made in class.

"I feel like I'm mining my house for cash. I'll need one bedroom set in an apartment, so I'm going to get my money back for all of it."

"Well, then what's the good news?"

"That is the good news."

Ben flinched.

She figured she knew what was coming. He'd tell her she couldn't move back in there even if her security system was Seal Team 6. She talked fast.

"Oh, by the way, I sold the house. The painters were done two days ago and Eleanor told the realtor it was ready. I guess upscale houses sell fast." Trudy was shocked at how fast it'd sold. "It went for enough to clear the loan with enough of a profit I'll get my down payment back. That will have to go straight to the IRS but it'll go a long way to getting that bill paid. The new owners take possession January first. So, I've got until New Year's Eve to find a place to live. That's four weeks." She'd been looking and there wasn't much she could afford. But the financial burden was easing. No more house payments. Her taxes coming under control. No more stunningly high home owner's insurance.

With her expensive accountant working overtime, the IRS was appeased once Trudy agreed to let them confiscate what was left after the house sold, and take every royalty check the second it came in the mail. They had tentacles into her bank account so they could snatch the money out without inconveniencing her one bit. Except for being broke of course.

Her professor's salary, well, she hadn't taken the job in this sweet, little Christian college for the money, but then she hadn't needed money. It wasn't exactly a pittance, but she'd yet to find a secure apartment building she could afford. When Eleanor refused her

November pay, she produced her own checkbook and stock portfolio that proved she had a lot more money than Trudy.

Trudy was putting the best face on it, but she was terrified to go back in that house. The fear was laced with guilt and failure. She was a reasonable woman. She knew he was dangerous, and she wouldn't shrink from locking him up. Turn the other cheek didn't mean you let a man beat you and kidnap you and terrorize you.

Did it?

But what if she'd tried harder to help him, right from the beginning? The defeat of all her high-sounding words pressed down on her heart.

"Selling the house is the bad news? I thought you wanted to sell it."

"No, that's not the second piece of news. I count it as part of the general news about the house. Sorry. I guess I have three pieces of news."

"What's the bad news." Ben seemed to brace himself.

"I'm sleeping at home tonight."

Trudy was glad they weren't going fast yet because he slammed on the brakes again.

"No, you're not."

"You can take me there if you want, or take me where ever you decide I should be, but I'll just call a cab and go home."

Ben didn't start driving. Maybe he was afraid his brakes couldn't take it.

Then he turned and studied her. She wasn't sure of her expression but it must've been bad because his annoyance faded.

"There's nothing wrong with just leaving now. Stay with Eleanor until you find a place. I can help you. I know this town. I know the best neighborhoods and the most secure apartment complexes. Staying safe isn't the same as letting Watson win. Just get out of that house right now and live somewhere he doesn't have a good spot to sit and watch you. We'll find a tall building and you can rent an apartment up high, with no tall buildings close. Then with some precautions, you can quit letting this maniac dominate your life. Yes, you have to be careful, but you don't have to give him the power to terrorize you. With God's help, you can find the strength…"

"God's help? Why would God help me, Ben?" Trudy turned to

him. "I've failed Him. All my talk—all my preaching about love—
and I *hate* that man. He's walking around free while I'm little more
than a prisoner, and I *hate* him."

"That doesn't mean you've failed God. This is just a tough time.
You'll come through it. Watson will make a mistake and violate his
restraining order. When he does, we'll be ready to arrest him. Or
he'll find someone else to torment."

"It's not just Watson. It's Liz. I open the mail, and all the bills
are past due. I look for apartments, and they're all out of my price
range. Big Deal Trudy Jennings, shivers in her ritzy house at night
because she can't afford to run her furnace."

Trudy's temper grew as she directed all the anger at herself. Ben
had driven to her house. She was surprised he hadn't fought her
harder. He pulled up to her door, lifted the console, turned and slid
halfway across the seat and rested his hand on her shoulder. "You
know I'm not going to let anything happen to you."

Trudy looked up. "I'm sorry for dumping on you this way. I
should be strong enough to handle this. It's just another way I'm
a failure."

"Everything's going to be okay. We're going to find you a place
to stay. Your money problems are going to iron out. And Watson is
going to move on to some other form of craziness. So, you don't
love him. No one would love him while he treated them like this."

"Jesus would."

Ben nodded. "Jesus does everything a lot better than we do. It's
fine to ask, 'what would Jesus do' but the bottom line is: He's so far
above us in His ability to love that we're only guessing what He
would do. You know something else? There's a difference between
righteous anger and hate. You're not failing. You're succeeding
against terrible odds."

Trudy shook her head. "You don't know the rage and pain in my
heart. The awful, vicious anger I feel."

"Wanna bet?" Ben arched an eyebrow.

Trudy didn't crack a smile. "I know that my soul is safe in Jesus
Christ. I know this doesn't separate me from my salvation. But it
makes me a failure in the very thing God called me to do. I've
become a Peter, denying Christ as soon as it got tough."

Ben laid a finger on her lips. "Is that the same Peter who went
on to be a great witness for Jesus? One of the great heroes and

great failures of Christianity, all wrapped up in one? A human being as much a sinner as any of us, and yet God used him to do great things? You *should* compare yourself to Peter. He did so much good, and you do, too."

Trudy caught his hand and pushed it away. "I know all that. Peter denied Christ and he heard the cock crow at sunrise and recognized his sin and repented. But I feel as if dawn is a thousand years away. I'm not even close to accepting my failure and restoring my ministry."

Ben reached for her hand.

"Tru, I want you to know you're not alone." Ben leaned closer.

She needed his strength because she had none of her own, and that wasn't a fair burden to place on anyone. She turned away. "I'm quitting, Ben."

"Quitting what?"

"Everything. Writing books, teaching my class, living in Long Pine. I'm moving to live near my great aunt in Tampa, Florida. I'm going to take care of her. I've tried to serve God and instead, I've enriched myself. Now the money is gone and I'm being harassed by a lunatic."

She turned to face him. "It's forced me to take a hard look at myself. My life isn't about serving the Lord."

"Of course it is."

She shook her head. "I've been serving myself. I've gathered so many material things around me that I couldn't even keep track of them all."

"Liz cheated you."

"No." Trudy wasn't going to let herself off the hook. "I knew I had nice things. I didn't have any idea of the extent of the spending, but even that is arrogance. God is dealing with me through this money mess and Watson's stalking. God called me to serve him. I'm going to do it. My aunt is eighty-seven and she needs help. I'm going to move near her and serve God in a more personal way by caring for her through her last years."

"Tru, your money problems will iron out, and we'll get Watson."

"When he attacks me again?"

Ben didn't answer. Trudy appreciated that he didn't give her some soothing lie.

"He's escalating, the vandalism is proof of that. He can't be functioning beyond his harassment of you. In the meantime, you're safe. He can hover all he wants, but he can't get to you."

Trudy gave a cynical snort much like the sounds Ben had made in her classroom.

"Don't cut and run like this, Tru, it's beneath you."

"I'm going to ask the dean for a leave of absence effective immediately."

"What about your students?"

"They'll be better off with someone else. I don't have anything but platitudes for them."

"Jesus' words are not platitudes."

Trudy nodded. "His words aren't the problem. I am. I'm the hypocrite who stands in front of a class and spouts off about love while I'm carrying around a heart weighted down with hate."

A long silence stretched between them.

It was over. She would escape from more than Watson; she'd escape from her whole, worthless life. She'd failed God. She shouldn't expect things to turn out any differently.

"What about me, Tru?"

She looked up and saw from the deepened furrows on his forehead and the wounded look in his eyes that she'd hurt him. Their gazes locked.

"You'll be better off, Ben. I haven't done anything since we met except take. I don't have anything to give to my students, or my patients, or my friends."

His eyes narrowed. "Is that what I am? A student—a patient—a friend?"

She wanted to say no, and tell him how much he meant to her. She wanted to reach out and pull him into her arms, into her life. But this wanting came out of the weakest part of herself.

She grabbed for the door handle instead.

He got out and rounded the truck. Just before she reached the door, he caught her arm. Trudy looked up at him. He had a strangely confident smile, considering she'd done nothing to inspire any confidence.

"You're not going to move to some retirement village in Florida. You're not going anywhere."

He bent down and pressed his mouth against her lips. The kiss ended before she had a chance to stop him, before she could talk herself into not kissing him back.

"Let's go make sure the house is secure, and see if Eleanor has returned to your big pink palace." He shoved her gently but firmly into the house.

# CHAPTER TWENTY ONE

TRUDY DIDN'T GO STRAIGHT TO the phone and call in her resignation that night, nor over the weekend, nor the next week. She wasn't going to let Ben stop her, but she'd think of that kiss and put off her resignation. She could always quit later.

Sitting at her desk in the hour before her last class on Friday, she was grading year end term papers when her door swung open.

"Do you mind if I come in?"

Trudy's head snapped up. Ralph Watson stood in the door to her office. Her heart bounded into her throat and when she opened her mouth to scream, not a sound came out. *Where is Gordan? Why didn't he stop this man?*

Watson's hands came up. "Please, just hear me out. I mean you no harm."

*Stay calm. Stay calm.* "You don't expect me to...to believe that when you've perched in front of my house every day, Mr. Watson."

"Please, call me Ralph."

*Call me Ralph?* Hate swelled in Trudy's heart. The conflict inside her almost tore her apart. She hated this man. God called her to love him but she couldn't. *God, help me do what's right.*

If she couldn't turn the other cheek with the only person who had ever actually harmed her, then she was a hypocrite. God had called her to love when it wasn't easy. To cure the ills of the world to the best of her ability with love.

And now she hated. She'd failed God in her first real test.

But she refused to continue to be a blatant sinner.

She dragged breath into her lungs, forcing the words out that she knew God expected her to say.

"Very well, Ralph. Have your say."

Her mouth spoke the kind words, but her heart didn't feel kindness. The hate and fear were too strong.

Panic added, "I'm very busy. I'm due in class in a few minutes."

The lies slid out of her mouth too easily. With an hour before class, she wanted him to think she'd be missed if she didn't appear somewhere very soon.

"You're not in any danger from me." Ralph stepped into the room and reached for the door behind him.

"Leave it open." Trudy didn't like the apprehension she heard in her voice. She was in a building full of people in the middle of the day. Surely, he wouldn't hurt her.

But Watson's eyes took on a hungry look as if he fed on her fear. His hand dropped away from the door and came to stand just across her desk.

Trudy looked past him into her outer office and her stomach jumped. Where was Ethel? She'd been told never to leave the front office without getting a replacement.

Trudy swallowed hard and made her eyes relax when she looked back at Watson. She knew, then, that he had watched and waited for a time when she would be alone. *Had he hurt Gordan?*

Watson licked his fleshy lips. His fingers shook as he ran a hand through oily black hair that stubbornly drooped over his eyes.

Trudy noticed he was disheveled. He'd looked like this when he came at her in the parking lot, then he'd been clean and tidy when he came that time with his lawyer. Now it was as if he was in a descent again. His jacket was Brooks Brothers, but his white shirt was dirty. Even standing across the desk from her, she could smell old sweat and urine, like the homeless men Trudy had worked with during her student days. He hadn't shaved in weeks. His teeth were yellow and his dark, greasy hair hung until it nearly covered his red veined eyes

"So, you're an author, Ralph." Trudy thought the normal topic might break the tension in the room. "I've looked up your books. You're very successful."

Watson's eyes shifted like an animal caught in a cage. "That's one reason I wanted to talk to you. I love the written word and I think you're a master." He placed his fingertips on her desk and leaned over.

Dark curves of dirt shown beneath his overly long nails. His voice shook as if the sound carried through high tension wires. "As a fellow author, I thought you could help me. I know now that was presumptuous of me." He leaned closer and the acid smell nearly pushed Trudy out of her chair. She stayed where she was to keep the desk between them.

*Soft Answer. Soft Answer. C'mon Trudy, practice what you preach.* "Ralph, I'm sorry I can't help you." She tried to shake off her revulsion and fear, and deal with the man honorably. She forced herself to lean forward a bit and cancel out her retreating body language. "The kind of help you're asking for isn't within my power to give."

"I know that." Watson shook his head as if denying his own words.

"Listen to me, please." Trudy felt the peace of God settle on her and she almost reached for the man's grimy hands. "My methods include intensive, twenty-four-hour intervention by professionals. You would benefit from this program, but a woman can't be there for you the way you need."

Trudy thought of her agreement with Ben, but Ben wasn't a candidate for her intensive therapy. He just needed a healthy nudge once in a while. And maybe a whack or two with Eleanor's frying pan in a pinch.

Watson needed the whole shebang.

"Dr. Jennings, if you could even give me an hour or so of your time, once a day, during a free period. If I could talk to you...the love and understanding I feel flowing out of you inspires me. It makes me believe all things are possible."

"All things *are* possible with God. There are so many people who can help you find the inner peace you're missing and help you to trust in the love your Heavenly Father has for you."

"This isn't about God." Watson straightened away from the desk and clenched his fists. "This is about my wife leaving me."

God nudged her to be honest. "Your wife was in the hospital because you hit her."

"I shoved her." Watson jammed his hands in his pockets. He wasn't tall, but he seemed solid. If he wanted, he could keep her in here by force until her screams brought help, which would be a matter of seconds.

"I never intended for her to fall." His hands fisted in his pockets and his grizzled face turned red. "It wasn't my fault."

"It's physical abuse." Trudy wondered at the leading she felt to pursue this. It was obviously not helping Ralph to admit his wrongdoing or, more importantly, to leave her office. "Classic denial says 'it's not my fault.' Your actions put your wife in the hospital."

Watson's teeth gritted and his eyes flared.

But Trudy plowed on. "That tells me you've got a long way to go before you can be in any healthy relationship. And it tells me you would never take counseling well from a woman."

"You say my problem is with women. Who better to work with me than a woman I respect?"

"Don't play games with me. You're a literate, intelligent author who can manipulate words. I know how therapy works. A man who hits women doesn't respect them, and he won't respect a woman's counsel. It's absolutely out of the question. You can be helped. It's possible your relationship with your wife can be mended."

She'd uttered her first real lie there.

She leaned forward, even though she saw his eyes narrow with rage. "Let go of your anger and let me help you, through Dr. Pavil, to restore yourself to the loving man God created you to be."

"So, you won't help? You're going to abandon me just like every other woman I've ever known?"

"I *am* helping you, if you'll just let me."

Watson shook his head, looking like an enraged bull. Trudy didn't want him to charge so she decided to stop waving red flags. "Let me call the doctor right now. You can speak with him yourself."

Trudy reached for the phone.

"No!" Watson lunged forward and slapped his hand over the receiver and Trudy's hand.

Trudy pulled back, but Watson held her hand, pressed down on top of the phone. His stench caused her stomach to roil.

"You have to help me." His hand tightened on Trudy's. His fingers cut off her circulation. "*Give me what I want or I'll take...*"

The outer door swung open and Ethel walked in singing the old Tina Turner classic, "What's Love Got To Do With It?" at the top of her lungs as she did a snazzy little salsa dance over to her desk.

Watson released Trudy's hand with a low-pitched growl. Clenching and unclenching his hands, he worked his mouth, as if physically restraining the words he wanted to say.

Trudy started shaking, and she saw Watson studying her. He licked his lips as if he could taste her fear and thought it was delicious and wanted more.

"Ethel, would you please come in here?" Trudy's voice shook.

A sharp sideways jerk of his chin seemed to admit he was routed this time. With narrow eyes and a smug little smile, he said, "We haven't settled our business."

"My decision is final. I'm going to include what happened here today in my police report."

"What *did* happen here today? All I saw was another example of your unkindness to a man in need. I wonder how the press would handle a story about how unloving and selfish you are?" Watson arched a shaggy eyebrow. "Another time, perhaps?"

He brushed past Ethel as she came into the office, still dancing to the oldies.

"Whazzup, Trudy?" Ethel chomped away on a mouth full of gum as the outer office door slammed.

Trudy drew in a deep breath and said to the woman who had just saved her, "Whazzup is, you're fired."

Ethel drew herself up to her entire five foot two. "You can't fire me. I'm calling my cousin, Lloyd."

"The dean is your cousin?"

"That's right. We'll just see who stays and who goes."

All the fear and rage Trudy had controlled around Watson erupted on poor unsuspecting, incompetent Ethel. "Don't call him from this phone. I'm barring you from it and from this office. You *walk* over and tattle-tale on me. And be sure to take all your personal things with you because I'm not letting you back in here."

"I've wanted out of this stupid job anyway. I'm sick of working for such a nicey-nice wimp."

She walked to her desk, snarling insults at Tru as she packed up her belongings.

"And then," Trudy laughed, "I had to Heimlich Ethel because she swallowed a wad of gum that was about twice the size of her throat."

"But you didn't back down." Ben made her go over the whole story again while he drove her home. "That's great."

"It's awful."

"You were strong."

"I'm a bully. I'm the exact person I'm writing about. I need to check myself into my own program. Maybe Dr. Pavil will take me on."

Ben smiled. Tru-Blu was growing a real live spinal column. "You stuck to your guns, right? She's fired, for real?"

"Ben, I'm supposed to be helping you respond to people in a more loving way. In the months since we started your therapy..."

"It's really been just a couple months—well, three...and a half," he said, smiling.

"You have turned me into a tyrant."

"Tyrant? Yeah, whatever. I'm hiring your next secretary, Tru. You're not good at this."

Tru sniffed at him, which Ben decided was the same as agreeing. He'd make sure her next secretary had a black belt and a license to conceal carry. Oh, and her new *male* secretary was going to be way too old for her and happily married.

"While I'm referring myself to Dr. Pavil, I'll sign you up, too. And I'd better do it quick, before I join a karate league and start prowling the streets of Long Pine wearing a super hero costume and beating up street punks."

Ben chuckled. "Nothing wrong with knowing how to defend yourself. I could show you some self-defense moves. As far as prowling the streets, you need to pick your spots. Street punks can be..."

"I'm not going to prowl." When Tru bared her teeth, Ben didn't grin for fear she'd bite him. "I'm turning into a raving lunatic who takes her temper out on anyone who gets in her way."

Ben decided his plan was working nicely. "Did I tell you I apologized to Scott for hanging up on the captain? And I make coffee every day now."

"How's that working out for you?"

"We've had six guys ask for a transfer out of the precinct because my coffee is so bad, but still, it was polite of me to do it. I do that three-second thing ten times a day when someone asked me a question. Since you weren't around to blame, I just said, 'I'll have that to you by the end of the day.' I've been told to report to sick leave and a few wise acres keep telling me they'll drive me to the ER."

"You're really trying to be polite?"

Ben nodded. "And I'm going to keep it up. I can smell the promotion already."

"The money and status will be great, but the reason to do this is for yourself, to live a more Christ-like life."

"You said I should do it for the money." Ben snapped his eyebrows low, then caught himself. "Sorry, that wasn't nice, and you're right. I'm going to work on my motives. Of course, I want to live a Christ-like life."

Bickering with Tru was so much fun, he usually threw her words back at her without thinking about them. But this time, when he said it out loud, he was a little surprised to realize he meant it. What would Jesus do? He sure wouldn't bark at Yarrow, no matter how fun it was. He might not dedicate his life to toughening up Tru either. He might like Tru just as squishy and sweet as she'd been when the semester started.

Ben sighed. All this counseling was hard work. "Early this morning, I sent a couple of uniforms to ticket Watson and arranged to have the church that owns that parking lot complain about his presence there. He's not going to be able to hang around in that spot anymore. He'll find another one I'm sure, but for now, he'll be gone."

"What time was he ticketed?"

"Just after noon. I called the church then sent the uniforms over."

Trudy sighed. "I suppose that's what set him off."

Ben turned away from the busy interstate. "Set him off?"

"He came to see me today."

"What?" Ben's jaw clenched until he thought his teeth might crack. "You've spent all this time telling me about firing Ethel and you didn't mention *Watson*?"

"I knew I had to tell you, but I've been dreading it. You've been doing so well with your temper and this is going to make you mad."

Ben forced his whitened knuckles to remain in control of his vehicle on the multi-lane rush hour traffic. He glanced at her and saw her rigid muscles and the deep lines at the corners of her eyes that told him she was exhausted. He laid the insomnia at Watson's feet. Of course, it sounded like she'd suffered from that forever, but Watson made it worse.

"If he hurt you, I'll kill him." He looked back at the road and was surprised that someone wound so tight could manage a weak laugh. "What's funny about any of this?"

"If your therapy was a class, I'd say that last sentence would earn you an 'F'."

Ben exited and headed for Tru's posh neighborhood. "Tell me what he said."

"Only if you'll promise to react with love."

"To Watson?"

Tru held up one hand. "Yes, to Watson. At least while he's miles away and we're alone in this pick-up. Just do it for practice."

Ben took the exit to Tru's house and once on the surface streets he slowed to a stop at a light and looked at her. Beneath the tired, dark-circled eyes was a glimmer of what made Trudy Jennings so special. She believed all the stuff she spouted. She tried to love the world into being a better place. The least he could do was behave during what amounted to an acting lesson.

With a sigh that made it sound like he was exhausted too, Ben said, "Okay. Now what did the little creep...?"

"Ben!"

He grinned at her. "I mean," he said, fluttering his eyelashes in his best girly-man fashion. "Tell me about it, and let's figure out how we can help this poor lost soul."

Tru rolled her eyes. "Nicely done. Since you're in character, I'll tell you."

"And that's when you fired Ethel?"

Trudy noticed Watson wasn't across the street. She reached for the door handle, wondering if there was a chance in a thousand she could head right for bed and get some sleep. "Yes, I fired her. Heads are rolling around me like I'm Madame Dufarge. I'm telling you, Ben, it's a wonder I didn't phone Eleanor and fire her. And I love Eleanor."

Trudy jerked the door open and slid down to the pavement.

Why did men always have to buy vehicles that floated ten feet off the ground?

"She *is* a little bossy."

Trudy whirled around. "Don't you dare say a single hurtful thing about Eleanor. I won't stand for it."

"Gotcha." Ben laughed. "I love Eleanor, too. She's safe from me."

"I knew that." Trudy grumbled, "How can you laugh?"

"Because this is a great day."

"A great day? It's one of the worst days of my life."

"Yeah, sorry about that. But Watson violated the restraining order. I'll run him in as soon as I can get my hands on him."

"He'll just get right back out." Trudy admitted she was scared to death of Watson and so tired, her synapses fired like popcorn.

"Not this time." Ben skirted the pick-up and walked beside her toward the house. "Violating the order is a misdemeanor, but grabbing you when you tried to make a call is assault. holding you against your will, if we push it to the limit, that's kidnapping. And I'm picking the judge this time. I wonder if Mom could fill in here in Long Pine for a day this week? We'll get an arrest warrant and this time, it'll stick."

"You know, you don't have to come in."

"You know, I do."

Trudy knew he did. "You're right. We haven't worked much on your therapy. We've spent most of the time with me telling you my troubles."

"But I didn't go nuts and rave about your troubles, did I?"

"Well, you did call him a..."

"I mean for the most part. So that was my therapy for today."

Trudy was too tired to argue with him. As an experienced insomniac, she could sense that her body had had enough. Maybe she would sleep tonight.

She laughed when Eleanor met them at the front door with her skillet and a can of mace.

Ben kissed the housekeeper good-bye.

And Trudy was asleep as soon as her head hit the pillow.

Her last thought as she fell asleep was, *Oklahoma City should have been the capitol of Oklahoma, not Tulsa.*

# CHAPTER TWENTY-TWO

TRUDY DIDN'T QUIT HER JOB. Watson didn't get arrested. "He's dropped out of sight. He's on the run." Ben grumbled about it every day on their rides to and from work.

When Trudy and Eleanor moved back to the pink monstrosity, Trudy felt Watson's presence, even though he was no longer at the parking lot. Florida and an elderly great aunt sounded like heaven on earth.

She was still determined to quit and put some real space between herself, and Watson and more than that, her own failure. But it was mid-December, finals week was coming and so was her eviction date. She was just too busy to quit and move away.

She'd imposed on Eleanor for a while and the temporary situation suited Trudy. Abandoning the house and losing all her clothing and most of her personal possessions to Watson's vandalism had left her feeling lighter. Except for the weight of fear.

Now, with no house to make payments on and most of her possessions fitting in the suitcases she'd taken to Garrison's Thanksgiving, she had the option of picking up and running anytime she wanted.

Trudy had ruthlessly sold things in preparation for her move. Top quality used furniture was surprisingly valuable. It helped put Trudy on a good enough financial footing to pay her share of Eleanor's rent.

Trudy considered accepting some offers to go on the paid speaker circuit over the Christmas break. But she was too demoralized to believe her advice was worthy of air time.

When she'd moved home, Ben had given her the sweet, sentimental gift of mace, with orders to keep it right at hand, day and night. With her house stripped of almost everything, and Eleanor asleep to rest up for Trudy's moving day tomorrow, Trudy spent her last night in her home lying awake. She felt relatively safe with Watson on the run, Eleanor in the next room, chemical weapons at hand, and the security system in place.

With no hope for sleep anytime time soon, Trudy got up and paced, careful to keep her lights off, to stay away from the windows and to keep quiet…no reason Eleanor had to stay awake with her.

Trudy heard a sound she couldn't identity. And she was a woman used to the sounds of her house in the night.

It didn't repeat itself but she thought it might've come from Eleanor's room. Trudy's old room had been farther away from Eleanor. Was it possible her faithful housekeeper had nightmares and Trudy had never known?

She went to the door and opened it. Looking across the hall to Eleanor's bedroom, she saw the door just barely ajar.

Another sound came from that room.

Maybe.

It was too faint to be sure.

Trudy took an uncertain step, not liking the idea of invading Eleanor's privacy by looking in on her while she slept. But if she was having a nightmare bad enough to disrupt her sleep, maybe Trudy could help.

She reached for the knob and swung the door open. A light was on in the bathroom connected to Eleanor's bedroom and it cast enough light for Trudy to see Eleanor's eyes wide open, glazed with fear.

And then she saw the gag. Eleanor shook her head and struggled. Her hands were bound by ropes.

"Don't move Dr. Jennings." Ralph Watson stepped out of the darkness of Eleanor's room, a gun in hand.

The gun pointed at Trudy first, then it slowly swung toward Eleanor.

"No, don't hurt her."

A cold smile appeared on Watson's grizzled face. "If you go with me quietly, she won't be hurt." Watson's eyes rabbited around the room. He panted like a trapped animal, his head moving from side to side as if he hunted for…her.

He looked up and Trudy's heart stopped. She thought of her mace, and her cell phone, left on her nightstand.

His eyes locked on her and the wildness faded, replaced by a hungry look that terrified Trudy.

*"Give me what I want, or I'll take it."* He lunged at her and grabbed her arm.

She screamed and jerked away. She turned and ran. If she could get outside, he'd come after her and leave Eleanor alone and someone would hear her scream.

She neared the top of the stairs as Watson hit her from behind. "Give me what I want!"

He shoved her onto the carpeted stairs. Her arms flew up and broke her fall.

With a quick twist and a loud grunt, Trudy knocked Watson aside and scrambled to her feet. She practically dove down the stairs and was nearly down when Watson grabbed her arm and yanked. She whipped around, knocked into him and he tumbled toward her, they both rolled to the base of the stairs.

Wearing a long, navy flannel nightgown, her legs got twisted in the fabric and she fought her way to her feet.

Watson's heavy, fumbling hands clawed at her legs. "You're coming with me. *Give me what I want.*"

She tripped, rolled to her back and kicked wildly as Watson rose above her. She nailed him in the face with her heel. Watson snarled like a wounded animal.

Another kick landed lower. He collapsed backward as Trudy screamed with everything in her.

She shoved herself up. Watson lay between her and the front door so she raced for the kitchen door.

*"Give me what I want!"* Watson's voice, breathless, grew stronger as Trudy ran.

Dashing past her kitchen phone, she grabbed its cordless receiver. She could call 911 as soon as she put enough space between her and Watson.

The sturdy latch on the kitchen door fought her hands. Watson shouted, "I'll take it. I'll take it. *Give me what I want.*" His voice came nearer.

The lock released and she jerked the door open and darted onto her patio. Running across her yard to get away from the light that spilled outside through the doorway, she fell over one of the many decorative rocks landscaping the edge of her beach. The rock scraped the skin off her toes and grated across her ankles. She landed face down, eating a mouth full of sand. Crawling for a few seconds on her hands and knees, she glanced over her shoulder.

Watson's form appeared, dark and menacing, in her doorway. Trudy froze. Stifling her gasping breath, her chest screamed out in pain.

Watson grabbed the door frame and looked around the dark beach. She realized in her dark pajamas and half concealed by the stone, he couldn't see her. She waited, afraid to use the phone, afraid to even breathe as he scanned the beach.

"*Give me what I want*," he howled above the pounding waves. The dull gleam of the gray metal gun caught Trudy's eyes.

Her stomach twisted. The thought of Watson's brutal hands on her terrified her, but she realized she'd never gone so far in her daydreams as to wind up dead.

She looked at his savage face, the tattered clothes and the filth that came out of a disturbed mind. Trudy knew he was fully capable of pulling the trigger.

Watson caressed the gun like he was holding a kitten in his hand. As he stared out into the night, he stopped screaming at her and crooned, "*Give me what I want. Or I'll take it. I'll take it. I'll take it.*"

The words continued, barely audible over the crashing surf. A litany of madness.

Looking carefully left and right, he stepped outside. Did she dare stay where she was? If he turned away, even for a few seconds, she'd risk dialing the phone. She could keep the phone behind the rock, but the phone beeped when she dialed. Even over the rush of the pounding surf, she didn't know how far the sound carried. She didn't dare risk it right now. He was too alert. Despite his obsessive repetition of his demand, he held the gun with icy steadiness. And her position was only hidden by her stillness.

"Watson, turn around."

Trudy jumped at the deep voice coming from inside her house. *Ben!*

He appeared behind Watson on the far side of the kitchen island. It was the middle of the night. How had Ben known she needed him?

A thrill raced through her as she lay motionless on her belly on the sand. Ben was here. Everything would be all right. The intensity of the relief and joy sent a shudder through her that wracked her from head to toe.

Watson turned to the voice. As he moved, with his right side away from Ben, Watson slipped the gun back into the pocket of his tattered black trench coat. *Did Ben know Watson was armed? Had he seen the gun?*

Her joy turned to a terror more intense than when she'd confronted a lunatic in her home.

Trudy quickly dialed 911 while she watched Watson face Ben. Watson stepped back into the kitchen.

She heard Ben say, in a soft voice, "Let's talk about this, Mr. Watson. Let me help you."

Watson's hand went slowly to his pocket.

Without waiting for anyone to answer it, Trudy laid the phone aside, hoping the 911 operator would figure out there was trouble and send help.

Ben had come to save her. Now she cowered here in the dirt while he risked his life rather than just shoot this lunatic. Ben was trying to be the man Trudy had pressured him to be.

She studied Watson for seconds that seemed to stretch into eternity. All her life, she'd made it her personal crusade to return good for evil. She'd gained whatever self-respect she possessed by believing herself to be a Christian who loved first, last and always.

Now she was faced with the same choice she'd had in her office, only this time what she decided about love and hate meant more than her own sin. It could mean Ben's life. Did her faith stretch to forgiving a man intent on killing her...and Ben?

Watson's hand slid a fraction of an inch at a time into his trench coat pocket.

The seagulls screamed overhead.

*'Greater love has no one than this, that he lay down his life for his friends.'*

That, she heard. And that's what Ben was doing: laying down his life for her.

Trudy climbed to her hands and knees.

"Mr. Watson, you know you shouldn't be here. You're not thinking clearly." Ben watched Watson carefully, conscious of every move, including the hand easing into the weighted down pocket.

"She knows I need her help." Watson's voice was gruff and low, but as he spoke the sound grew higher pitched, fractured.

"She promised me. She didn't keep her promise. She needs to give me what I want. If she doesn't, I'll take it. I'll take it. I have to. It's her fault, not mine."

He'd been listening to Trudy all semester. He didn't want to resort to violence with Watson, that wasn't God's way. But when he heard Watson's ranting, something primal awakened in Ben that made all his usual anger pale by comparison.

Ben fought down the hate. *A soft answer. A soft answer.* It was a sin to hate Watson the way he did right now. *God, help. I don't feel any love for this man at all.*

Then something miraculous happened.

His furious, murderous heart didn't win. God did. And Ben knew what he had to say.

"God loves you, Ralph."

A mumbling Watson stepped further into the kitchen. A large island stood between them.

Flecks of foam sprinkled the corners of Watson's mouth. His unshaven face was haggard. His whole body sagged as if under the weight of his hatred of everything and everyone.

With those miraculous words, sent by God, peace washed through Ben. He never took his eyes off Watson. All his cop instincts were on high alert, but he felt the power of God flowing through him. This is what was at the heart of turning the other cheek, this knowledge of the love of God. The protection of a soul through faith in Jesus Christ.

Ben understood for the first time that Watson couldn't hurt him. Even in death, God would protect Ben's soul.

"It's the strangest thing, Ralph. Knowing how much God loves you fixes everything. If everyone could just tap into that love, no one would be angry. No one would hurt another human being. There wouldn't even be hunger or poverty because we'd be sharing everything."

Watson's left hand rested on the countertop of the island. Ben saw what seemed like detached madness in the man. He doubted if Watson even understood him.

"God will forgive your sins if you just ask. He knows the anger that boils inside you. He can heal it. He can replace it with peace. How long has it been since you've known peace, Ralph?"

Some of the glazed look faded from Watson's eyes. "Peace?" The word seemed laced with scorn. "There's no peace in this world. The strongest win. The strongest take. That's life."

Ben had reached Watson's fracturing mind enough to communicate, but he knew the man was dangerous. Even talking in ways that made sense, the fury boiled out.

Watson's right hand disappeared into his coat pocket. Ben let his arms hang loose at his sides, his gun tucked into a holster in the middle of his back. God stayed his hand and gave him more words.

"I forgive you, Ralph."

Watson's hand stopped moving and came into view as he gripped the counter. "Forgive me? For what? I haven't done anything to you."

"You've made someone I care about feel terrible. You left her bleeding and terrified in a parking lot. You made her fear the phone and the mail and the dark. You harassed a sweet lady who only wants to help people. You hurt her and taught her some cruel lessons about how hard it can be to love others."

Ben took a step toward him. "She's not as innocent as she was before she met you and that's a terrible loss. Her joy in living was a great gift to the world. But, even though you've done all that, I still forgive you."

"I don't want your forgiveness." Watson's voice chilled Ben with its artic hate.

Dark greasy hair framed Watson's eyes as they lost focus.

"You have it anyway, Ralph." Ben remembered Trudy advising they should call her stalker by his first name. Ben bit back a smile. Trudy had been right about that, too. She'd been right about everything.

"It's not a gift you have to receive. It's freely offered whether you want it or not."

"Well, I've got something to offer you." Watson dropped his hand and produced a 9 mm Glock. Ben had his gun in his hand before Watson's cleared the island.

Ben leveled his gun, hating what he had to do. His finger tightened on the trigger.

A dull thud drew Ben's attention away from Watson's rising weapon.

Watson's eyes crossed. His mouth sagged open and the gun fell below the countertop just before Watson sank out of sight.

Trudy stood behind him holding a decorative stone. Trudy's eyes followed Watson's fall. She bent over, pulled the gun away from him, and laid it on the countertop as if she were touching a rattlesnake.

Ben picked up Watson's gun and flicked on the safety. He tucked his own weapon into the small of his back and came around the island to stand beside Trudy.

Trudy gave Ben the most relaxed smile he'd ever seen on her face. She bent over her tormentor's still form and said, "I forgive you, too, Ralph."

# CHAPTER TWENTY-THREE

ELEANOR STOOD IN THE DOORWAY to Trudy's kitchen, wringing her hands. Trudy thought she was a vision in a bright blue sweat suit and sponge curlers. "Are they going to lock him up this time?"

"I want my lawyer," Watson snarled as he fought against the cuffs. "I know my rights." He sat on the hall floor, hands secured behind his back. He'd regained consciousness before the ambulance arrived and along with a lawyer he was fighting the medical examination.

Trudy had untied Eleanor and they'd gotten back downstairs, dressed now, about the time the first patrol car showed up. A crime scene unit was hard on their heels. Since they had Trudy and Ben as witnesses, and Watson cuffed and waiting, there wasn't much to investigate. They now waited for the lawyer that Watson demanded non-stop at the top of his lungs.

Trudy gave Watson a nervous glance. "Of course, they're going to lock him up. We caught him red-handed. Didn't we, Ben?

Ben had finished briefing the CS Unit, which then busied itself spreading fingerprint dust all over the house.

Eleanor crossed her arms and scowled. "We have to vacate by tomorrow. I've got to clean this mess up."

Trudy glanced at the wall clock. "You mean by today."

Ben grunted. "No way he walks. We already had a warrant out for him, which he's been hiding from, which makes him a flight risk. He violated the restraining order; and B&E is a felony. And as a convicted felon, he's not allowed to own a gun, another felony. He threatened you with it, and worst of all..."

Ben grinned at Trudy until she wanted to smack him. Or maybe hug the daylights out of him. She hadn't found out yet how he'd managed to show up in the nick of time.

"Worst of all what? What can be worse than threatening to kill me?" Trudy's eyes widened, "Well, except for succeeding, of course."

"He tried to kill *me*, a police officer. No way he gets bail."

Trudy frowned. "Why is it worse to shoot at you than me?"

"I've never understood that myself." Ben shrugged. "But it is."

Eleanor cleared her throat. "It *is* worse. As an officer of the law, Ben stands for justice, for order, for security."

"Don't forget truth and the American way," Ben interjected.

"I want my lawyer," Watson shouted as he struggled against the cuffs, as if he thought his civil rights could break tempered steel.

"When an officer of the law is attacked, the perp isn't just committing a crime; he's attacking the defenders of the law." Eleanor quit wringing her hands enough to sound indignant. "If criminals do that with impunity, we'd have anarchy. And that's why it's considered a more serious crime."

Ben rolled his eyes. "I just think it makes other cops mad. I'll bet, right now, every college professor who's heard about this is mad on Tru's behalf. But professors don't work a night shift, so not that many have heard about it. Plus, they don't have cool radios to spread the word. And, since professors don't carry guns on their hips, you don't notice it so much when they're upset."

"You're violating my rights. I just wanted to talk to her." Watson twisted his body and lunged at Trudy.

A uniformed officer caught Watson by the shoulder before he even made it to his knees and pushed him down. "Let's load him in the cruiser, Detective Garrison. He's a pest."

"Leave him there for now." Ben nodded at the floor. "I'd like to see his lawyer myself."

Ben turned to Trudy. "You seem different, like you're not so furious at Watson anymore."

Trudy nodded. "The weight is gone. I'm not sure why."

"Even the anger at Liz? Or do you want to find her and whack her over the head with a rock, too?"

"I think I'm over Liz."

"The money's not going to matter anyway."

"You're right. I think I can finish my book now. The advance plus selling everything I can, will clear all my debts, including the IRS, and allow me to rent an apartment."

"That's great, but that's not why your money problems are solved." Ben looked like he wanted to hum.

The night had been good. Watson couldn't lawyer his way out of this, and Trudy's writer's block was over. "Why do you think they're solved?"

"Because you're going to sue Watson for every penny he's worth."

"I'll kill you before you get a dime of my money." Watson roared and sprang at Trudy again.

The uniformed officer grabbed his shoulder. "Keep it up, buddy. You're resisting arrest and making terroristic threats."

"Could you send him to Guantanamo Bay with the other terrorists?" Eleanor scowled at Watson. "I hear it's really hot down there."

"Do you think I should sue him?" Trudy tried to keep the gleam of greed out of her eyes. It suited her to get a little revenge. She didn't want his disgusting money earned with those nasty books, but giving a woman all his money would punish Watson as much as a life sentence.

"I think you and his wife and anybody else who can think of an excuse should sue him." Ben's brows arched and he grinned. "I might get in line myself. He pointed a gun at me. I might be traumatized. I might not be able to work."

"Cool it, Garrison." Scott came in. "You're sounding more like a wimp every day."

Trudy smiled. Her counseling must be working if Ben sounded like a wimp.

"Why are you so cheerful?" Ben asked Trudy. "I mean, I know it felt good to paste this nutcase..."

Watson crouched on the hallway tile, growling and glaring.

"What happened to the anger and guilt over not forgiving or loving him? I'd think whacking him would have made that worse."

"You'd think." Trudy shrugged. "I realized something, when I knew I had to stop him from hurting you."

"What?" Ben smiled at her. "How much you like me."

"No."

Ben's smile faded.

"I do like you. That's just not what I realized."

Ben continued to watch her.

"The thing is, there are different ways to love somebody. I can turn the other cheek all day long, but if Ralph isn't going to stop hurting me, then I have to take steps to ensure my own safety. Once he's confined, he can get all the counseling his fortune..."

"What's left of it after you and his wife are done with him," Ben reminded her.

"He scared the living daylights out of me, too." Eleanor smiled like Ebenezer Scrooge before the ghost of Christmas future.

Ben grinned at her. "Good girl."

Trudy needed to say this, in front of both of them. "God used force, through me, to get Ralph's attention and put him in a place where he has no choice to but seek help."

Still grinning, Ben looked at Watson. "You'll have plenty of time to seek help, buddy. I count four felonies here tonight."

"Six," Scott said. "With the three strikes rule, Watson isn't stalking anybody for the rest of his life. Well," Scott winked at Ben. "Not anybody without a rap sheet. I guess he could stalk other convicts."

Scott looked down at the growling, struggling Watson. "Be careful stalking the lifers, though. They hate that."

A uniform walked inside. "He's got two more weapons in the car and one of them has been linked to some street crime. I suppose he might've knocked over a couple of convenience stores but more likely he gained possession of it through illegal means, plus he's a felon, so if he's been consorting with other felons to gain illegal access to the weapons..."

"That's eight." Ben gave the enthusiastic kid a thumbs–up. "He's so completely nailed."

"And this is Texas. So, he'll spend his life in prison," Eleanor said, eyes bright.

The nicest feeling swept through Trudy: sleepiness. "He can get all the intensive personal counseling he wants. Me bashing him with that rock made that possible."

"I think I see another book in this approach, Tru–Blu. Tru Interventions: Rock."

Trudy laughed at Ben. "I'm outlining it in my head even as we speak."

"Maybe we oughta find Liz. Knocking a little sense into her

would do you a world of good."

Trudy tilted her head as she considered it. "Maybe we should."

"You've created a monster, Ben," Eleanor scolded.

"How did you come to be in my house tonight anyway?" Trudy asked.

Ben opened his mouth.

"We need a statement." Scott slapped Ben on the arm. "Quit flirting and get to work." Scott grabbed Watson by the shirt front and hauled him to his feet. "We've got work to do at the station-house."

"I'm not leaving without my lawyer." Watson scowled as Scott lugged him toward the door.

Ben turned to Eleanor. "Would you excuse us, Eleanor? Tru and I need to talk."

"I'll start cleaning up this mess." Eleanor marched away, muttering about what a mess dusting for fingerprints made.

Ben rested his hand on Trudy's arm and gestured her toward the living room.

"You were going to tell me how you came to be in my house." Trudy looked around the perfectly proportioned room. It had been fun living in such a beautiful house. She sat on a folding chair.

"No, I wasn't."

"You weren't?" Exhaustion hit Trudy hard, as if seeing Watson arrested had relaxed her enough to sleep.

"No, I was going to ask you how we could end all our official relationships."

Trudy jerked fully awake. "You want to end our relationship?" She heard the dismay in her voice and tried to recover some poise. "I mean, not that we have a relationship."

Ben smiled a sad smile. "Tru, darlin', we've got so many relation-ships, I have to take off my shoes to count them all."

Trudy smiled.

"We're teacher and student."

"You're getting a really good grade, Ben. I've been meaning to tell you, your term paper..."

"Later, Dr. Jennings." Ben sat in a chair next to her. "We're police and crime victim."

"That one's about over." Trudy held herself upright as the weight of her fear eased a little more. "Thank heavens."

Ben nodded and scooted his chair next to her. "We're doctor and patient."

Trudy tilted her head a little. "Technically, I don't think we ever managed that. You never paid me."

"And I was never *that* patient."

Trudy turned to him, smiling. "You were a great patient. You've made changes that have improved your life. You were easy to help because your problems weren't rooted in pathology."

"Rooted in pathology?"

"That means you weren't enough of a flake to be a real test."

Ben shrugged. "Sorry."

"You never had the dysfunctional proclivities inherent in the truly..."

Ben put his hand over her mouth. "Please, not at this hour of the night."

Trudy nodded behind Ben's gentle hand.

He stopped touching her, and she missed it.

"So, I'd say that almost every possible relationship we have makes it illegal for me to ask you this next question."

*Illegal?* She wished he'd put his hand back.

She leaned close. "I promise not to call a cop."

Silence stretched between them.

He grinned at her.

"What's the question?" She waited.

He kissed her.

When she could talk again, she said, "That wasn't a question."

"Oh, yes, it was."

Trudy narrowed her eyes at the impossible man. "Then here's the answer." She kissed him back.

He smiled. "Just the answer I was hoping for." He leaned toward her.

"Do we need a chaperone in here?" Eleanor wielded a bucket and rag.

Ben stood. "I think maybe we do." He held out his hand and tugged Trudy to her feet. "I need to go. It'll take all night to book Watson, so get some sleep, Tru-Blu."

He almost got away before she asked, "But what were you doing in my house?"

Ben left without answering.

Eleanor and Trudy exchanged a glance.

"Any chance you can get some rest now?" Eleanor looked doubtfully at the smeared-up mess the crime scene techs had left behind.

"I might." Trudy looked up the long staircase. This was the last time she'd sleep here—or lay awake here, as the case may be. "I'm going to try. I've got class in the morning."

"And I'll start cleaning."

"You should get some sleep, too, Eleanor."

Eleanor patted Trudy's arm. "I'm good. One long night won't hurt me. The new owners are supposed to arrive at ten in the morning. Then I'm done with this place. You'll get up and go to work. I'll go home and sleep all day."

"I should stay and help, but I'm out on my feet." She reached for the banister and noticed her hand trembling. "I think I'm crashing from adrenaline overload."

Eleanor wrapped a stout arm around Trudy's waist and helped her up the stairs. As sweet Eleanor tucked her into bed, Trudy was aware, in the way only an insomniac can be, of the fuzziness in her brain that signaled impending sleep. She said a prayer as her mind shut down.

Her last thought was, "What was Ben doing in my house?"

# CHAPTER TWENTY-FOUR

"SO, WHAT WERE YOU DOING at my house last night?"
Ben rested a wrist on the steering wheel, pleased that it hadn't occurred to her to call a cab to get to work. He remembered how long and hard she'd objected to riding with him at first. He wasn't about to remind her she was safe. He liked carpooling with Tru-Blue Jennings.

He glanced at her classy outfit. Designer stuff—he remembered it from Thanksgiving. Gray slacks and a white blouse with a black, gray and white plaid blazer. Her hair was tidy in its usual clip at the base of her neck. She had tiny gold balls in her ears and a single gold chain around her neck. Nothing fancy, just perfect.

Or maybe the outfit just went out of its way to look perfect and expensive because it was lucky enough to get to hang around Tru.

Since he didn't want to answer her question, he announced, "I got word this morning that I'm being promoted to Detective First Grade."

Tru turned around, her face radiant in a big smile. "I saw you on the news this morning, standing next to the mayor when he announced it. That's a two grade jump, isn't it?"

"Yep." He wheeled his truck onto the interstate. He knew the way to the university like the back of his hand. "They said I was long overdue, said it like, Shazaam, how'd we overlook you for so long. I'm getting a commendation, too. Not specifically for this case but for my overall record."

"Wow." Tru reached over and patted his arm. "You really benefited from my counseling, then. It really helped you."

He controlled his squinting eyes, or at least he didn't turn them on her. "I'd like to think arresting Watson had something to do with it. It's a high profile bust. Stalking is always a tough case to make, and I did it."

Tru shrugged. "It helped that he managed to override my security system, break into my house, attack us both with a handgun—oh and tying Eleanor up, that counts as what? Taking a hostage? Assault? Kidnapping?"

Waving a hand, Ben said, "Probably all of that."

"After that, it wasn't such a tough case to make."

Ben wanted to remind her he'd saved her life. Sure, she saved him back, but his original rescue seemed to have gotten lost in the shuffle somehow—the shuffle in Tru's head, at any rate.

At least they'd noticed down at the precinct. Ben decided it was beneath him to beg for compliments, especially since he'd just gotten a sweet raise.

"The mayor talked about how there's no such thing as *'rich man's justice'* in good old Long Pine," Tru added. "He sounded pretty proud of himself when he said money wouldn't buy Watson out of trouble."

"As if his money didn't do exactly that when we first brought him in months ago."

"It had to look good for him politically to announce your promotion right there on the morning news."

It pinched a little that she'd given herself the credit for his promotion and now she was throwing more credit toward the mayor's political calculations. But he was in a chipper mood so he didn't pursue it.

"I liked the part where he insinuated O.J. Simpson would've been convicted in this town."

"Tough talk." Tru snickered. "And of course, Watson attacking in my neighborhood didn't hurt. It was like a slug fest between two financial forces of nature. Cullen Heights—that's me with my lake house—versus the Bourne neighborhood where Watson lives. If this had happened in the gang infested area on the south side of town, no one would have turned a hair."

Ben looked at her out of the corner of his eyes. "We've done some good work reining in the gangs."

Tru patted him again.

She wasn't paying the right kind of adoring attention to him this morning. Ben thought of pulling over and giving her a good morning kiss. That would get her attention. "You know we didn't really settle anything last night."

"Which reminds me, what were you doing at my house last night?"

Ben tried to be casual when he hunched one shoulder. He'd hoped she'd forget about that in all the chaos. Since confession was good for the soul, he said, "I've been sleeping on your beach."

"What?" She jerked forward so hard her seatbelt locked. She twisted around to face him. "Sleeping on my beach?"

Ben nodded. "I knew Watson was escalating and I wanted to be on hand if he freaked out."

"You told me he was on the run. You said I didn't have to worry so much."

"You didn't. I was worrying for you."

"Ben, for heaven's sake, it's freezing outside."

Ben curled up one corner of his mouth and controlled a shiver. "Tell me about it."

"How long has this been going on?"

"Since the first night he was parked across from your driveway."

Tru counted. "That's weeks." She stared out the window, then glanced at him as if she were a little afraid. "It's rained."

"Much as I hated the idea, I was really rooting for him to crack up and attack you."

"Ben!"

"Well, I was freezing! I don't know if I'd have lasted much longer." He would have. Dynamite couldn't have blasted him off that beach as long as Tru was in danger. "Of course, I did have an insulated sleeping bag, a waterproof tent and thermal everything."

"How'd you haul all that in with you?"

"It's been stored in your garage the whole time." Ben frowned at her. "Eleanor knew. You aren't very observant."

Tru rolled her eyes. "I'm not used to being a crime victim."

"Nothing wrong with that. Then tonight I didn't even see him go in. We found his laptop and he had the code to your security system. I found a note with your handwriting in his car with the code written down. I guess he got it the night he vandalized the place."

"You know, you don't have to drive me to work anymore."

Ben nodded. Rats! She was using her brain again. "So, instead of riding with me to work because you have to..." Ben sent her his most charming smile. "How about riding with me because you want to?"

He pulled into a parking space.

Tru unbuckled her seatbelt and grinned. "I do want to."

Glad to be done driving so he could look only at Tru, Ben cut the engine and turned toward her. "I'd like you to have dinner with me."

Tru turned her baby-blues on him. "You mean like a date?"

Ben let the silence stretch as they looked at each other. Not cop and victim, not doctor and patient, not teacher and student. "I mean *exactly* like a date."

Tru watched him for a long time. Ben enjoyed the scrutiny but, as the seconds ticked by, he started to get nervous. Always thinking, this woman. "Or we could just keep carpooling, if you're not ready to do something like..."

Tru leaned across the long bench seat and kissed him.

It was just as well. He was afraid if his mouth was unoccupied he was going to do something pathetic, like beg.

When Tru straightened away from him, he asked, "Is that a yes?"

"That's a yes."

"Aren't you afraid hanging around with me will make you want to whack more people on the head with a rock?"

Tru flinched. "I never did anything like that before we met."

"You never did anything like that before you met Watson either. I'm thinking we hang the blame for all of that on him."

Tru grinned and, with a tiny shrug, said, "Fair enough. And I don't even have to sue Watson, because my money problems are solved."

Ben straightened away from her. "I didn't hear of a bank robbery over the police band. How'd you solve your money problems?"

"I finished Tru Interventions: Bullies."

"You didn't sleep at all?"

"Yes, I slept like a baby. By the time the police left, it was almost dawn, but I got three solid hours of sleep."

"Then how'd you finish your book?"

"I dreamed it."

"Did you walk in your sleep and type it, too?"

"Nope." Tru slid closer to him and grabbed one of his hands. "But I dreamed of the ending, exactly how it should be. I can type it up tonight and send it off tomorrow."

"You found a way to give a soft answer to bullies, too?" Ben tried to keep the skepticism out of his voice.

"A soft answer does turn away wrath."

Ben nodded. "I've got the promotion to prove it."

Since she was holding his hand, he tugged her a little closer. "I owe that to you, Tru. You were right. A lot of the people I work with used to be my friends. They used to talk about their day and relax around me. Then I became a grouch and they started avoiding me. Worse than hurting my career, it was hurting my friends and my faith. I learned all of that from you."

"And I took using a soft answer to turn away wrath too far." Tru looked down at their joined hands, then raised her chin. "I'd become a liar."

Ben brushed her hair away from her face. No scars from Watson's first attack. She was healed and her terror was finally over.

"You're the most honest woman I know." Ben cupped her cheek. "You told me some things I didn't want to hear."

Resting her face on Ben's hand, she said, "I was honest with you, but I let everyone around me walk all over me. Liz and her unkindness. Ethel and her laziness. I need to speak softly, but I need to be honest, too."

Ben nodded. "You can't have any real power if you don't speak the truth."

"And how can I write about Tru Interventions if there's no truth? From now on, I'll speak the truth in love. I'll use a soft voice, and I'll still turn the other cheek, but I won't quietly let people get away with sin either."

Ben shrugged, wondering if the playgrounds of America would ever be the same. "It sounds simple, but something tells me it won't be. I hope it's worth all you went through to learn this lesson."

"It's the message God wants me to share. I'll finish the book tonight and have the advance check by next week."

"And Watson's wife is divorcing him, so she'll get half of everything. Thanks to a very subtle hint on my part, Watson just hired a new personal manager." Ben was silent, waiting for her to add two and two together.

She didn't disappoint him. "No," she breathed, her eyes wide.

"Yep. He hired Liz this morning to handle his business affairs while he's in jail. I did some quick footwork to secure his wife's half of the estate before Liz spent it all."

Tru laughed too hard to ask any more questions for a few moments. She swiped under her eyes and chuckled. "He can't wear Armani in prison, can he?"

"She'll no doubt stack his closets full of it, until she spends so much he loses his house."

Tru giggled again. "Then everything is fine."

"Yep and since you're going to be spending every spare minute with me, I think you'll be so happy, the insomnia will disappear. So, all your problems will be solved, thanks to me."

"I've always had insomnia. It didn't start when Watson attacked me. I sleep less than five hours a night, then occasionally crash on a Saturday and sleep for twelve hours straight. But it's not all bad. I've written most of my books at night. Having insomnia has made me tired, but rich."

"Rich, but broke."

Tru nodded. "Just think how broke I'd be if I *weren't* rich."

Ben jabbed his index finger toward the Psycho building. "Get to work, Tru-Blue. The final is tonight and then we're no longer student and teacher. Right after class, we'll grab something to eat. This is a real date, so don't ask Eleanor to tag along."

"She's my roomie, now," Tru said in a wheedling voice that didn't match the gleam of mischief in her eyes. "We really ought to invite her."

"No." Ben leaned close, cupped her face, and kissed her. A real kiss. One that made promises.

Tru rested her forehead against his and turned her cheek into his palm. "But what about your hero complex? Eleanor does hero worship better than I do."

"My hero complex has always been attracted to softies. And you're no softy, Tru. You're one tough cookie. You saved my life."

"I think your other girlfriend wanted the hero. She didn't look deep enough to see how wonderful you are under the shining armor."

He heard her kindness and saw her glowing eyes, focused strictly on him, and had to bite his tongue to keep from asking her to give him a very soft answer to the questions, 'Do you love me? Will you marry me? Will you have my children?'

He gave her an enthusiastic kiss good-bye which she returned with interest. She got out and headed into the Psycho building. When she glanced back at him, he gave her a jaunty wave and pulled out of the parking lot.

He'd save those questions for their second date.

# MARY CONNEALY

## *Author of Romantic Comedy with Cowboys*

MARY CONNEALY WRITES ROMANTIC COMEDY with cowboys often with a strong suspense thread. She is a two time Carol Award winner, and a Rita, Christy and Inspirational Reader's Choice finalist.

Mary has written 55 books in print including her latest, The Accidental Guardian for Bethany House Publisher, book #1 of the High Sierra Sweethearts series.

She's writing (and sometimes reading) when she should be cooking! Then someone (her cowboy husband) comes in and is hungry! So she's got a whole lot of fast recipes to choose from in her cookbook Faster Than Fast Food.

Mary is the wife of a Nebraska cattleman, a life that gives her special insight into ranch life.

### FIND MARY ONLINE AT:
www.maryconnealy.com
www.seekerville.blogspot.com
www.petticoatsandpistols.com
www.maryconnealy.com/series-guide

# MARY CONNEALY BOOKS